Sophie a  ntastic
Feathered Fables

Beyond the Veil
Quest for the Samhain Treasure

Curtis Lind

EXPLORA BOOKS
700 – 838 West Hastings St. Vancouver, BC V6C 0A6
www.explorabooks.com
Phone: (604) 330 6795

No part of this book may be reproduced, stored in a retrieval system, or transmitted by any means without the written permission of the author.

Because of the dynamic nature of the Internet, any web addresses or links contained in this book may have changed since publication and may no longer be valid. The views expressed in this work are solely those of the author and do not necessarily reflect the views of the publisher, and the publisher hereby disclaims any responsibility for them.

ISBN: 978-1-83430-126-6 (*Paperback*)
978-1-83430-127-3 (*Hardback*)

© 2025 by Curtis Lind. All rights reserved.

Table of Contents

Act 1

- A Mysterious Invitation 1
- The Scarecrow and the Cryptic Map 7
- The Whispering Woods 12
- The Pumpkin Graveyard 16
- The Scarecrow's Tale of Samhain..................... 23
- and the Goddess Pomona 23
- A Ghostly Gathering and Crooked Straw........ 27
- A Conflict Within 32
- The Betrayal and a Badger 35

Act 2

- The Vex Shadows and a Trail of Trust 42
- The Hidden Chamber of Time.......................... 47
- The Badger's Birthright 53
- A Tryst with Treachery..................................... 59
- A Tough Lesson.. 63
- The Ancient Crystal 71

Act 3

- The Red Feather... 78
- Cloudy With a Chance of Showers................... 83
- Lost 90
- The Abandoned Mansion 95
- The Reunion 101
- The Plan 105
- The Chamber.. 109
- Hollow Hills and the Sídh 116

- About the Illustrator 125
- About the Author... 127

A Mysterious Invitation

Their gray wings drooping, beaks hanging open in hopes of cooling themselves, the two birds perched high in the tallest branches, towering above the trees and bushes that surrounded their beloved home, Babu Nyumbani. Called Babu for short, the parrots cherished their special home. Babu was no ordinary tree; he held secrets inside his massive, gnarled trunk and ancient limbs. While weary travelers rested in his branches and above his roots, he quietly gathered their stories, wishes, and dreams. He held them tightly, hoping to share them. Over the years, secret journey branches sprouted where the travelers rested, giving passage to incredible and magical adventures for his two feathered residents.

Under a sweltering African sun, the vast rainforest of the Congo unfolded, a green tapestry painted with blistering heat. As October days passed, fires were kindled across fields, echoing an ancient tradition of incinerating the old to make way for the new, clearing the fertile soil of remaining crops and rampant undergrowth.

The still air was filled with ordinary bird chatter, a distant rustling of leaves, and that hazy smokey scent like a campfire that spread throughout the valley. From the

Congo River to the highest mountains in the North, the thick smokey haze could be seen and smelled.

It felt like time had slowed to a crawl in the heat as most of the animals that called the rainforest home sought out shade and settled down for an afternoon nap.

That was until an unusual, ragged old envelope arrived. Adorned with gleaming silver threads that reflected the bright sunlight and eerie orange markings. It was the beginning of a mysterious day at the enchanted tree-home of two African Gray parrots, Sophie and Pierre.

"Sophie! Look what's fallen from the sky!" Pierre squawked, flapping his wings with eagerness. The younger of the two siblings, his bright green eyes gleamed with curiosity as he peered at the peculiar envelope caught in the branches.

Sophie, older and always more cautious, fluttered down from her perch and joined Pierre. Her beak curved into an intrigued grin as she pecked open the envelope. "An invitation?" she echoed. Her eyes widened as she read aloud, "By order of the Roman goddess Pomona, Empress of the Festival of Samhain, your presence is required, and so, you are herewith invited to a Haunting Halloween Celebration!" A squeaky gasp echoed through the silence.

"Halloween Party!" Pierre whooped, his eyes squeezed tight with excitement, dancing up and down on his branch such that he almost fell off.

"But where is it?" Sophie wondered aloud, tilting her head in thought as a gentle breeze rustled the envelope.

A second faded and tattered parchment slipped out, unfurling to reveal a treasure map.

"Well, I'll be a Red-Rumped Tinkerbird!" Pierre gasped; his eyes wide with awe.

"It's a treasure map!"

And time stopped. Sophie hesitated. Their life in the rainforest was a safe, predictable routine outside of the journey-branch adventures they'd experienced before.

This was new, and new could mean danger. Her thoughts raced back to that memorable day before they found their home, etched in her memory as if it were yesterday.

With Pierre in tow, they fluttered around the rainforest chasing after their goal, a search for the tastiest fruit known to exist. It was a toss-up between the hard-shelled Baobab fruit or Sophie's favorite, a juicy mango. With the meal in sight, the birds landed near the ripest fruit on the tree. Today, it was Baobab. The two birds used their beaks to open the hard shell and dove in. After her third piece, the weight of the meal settled in her stomach, she felt overstuffed. As she watched as Pierre slurp up the last of number four and get ready to pounce on number five, she cleared her throat, nodded at his now descending stomach, and recommended they return home. He grinned and agreed. It was a difficult flight for him and his swollen belly.

As twilight began to descend, it cast long eerie shadows that made the familiar forest seem almost alien. Arriving back at their perch, the usual noise and warmth of their family were missing. Their branch, empty. Pierre's calls echoed into the now quiet evening and went unanswered. Nothing. The birds realized that to look for them in the dark forest was not a good idea. They had both learned that being lost in the African night is no picnic. In the earliest of the dawn's light, the next day when the shapes of the surrounding rainforest appeared, a pang of fear began to creep into their hearts. Did their family desert them? Returning late that afternoon, exhaustion weighed on their wings from flying all day. Pierre's eyes mirrored the fear Sophie herself felt. Their family was nowhere in sight or sound. The chilling thought began to solidify in her mind. Abandoned. "It can't be," thought the fair young bird. "They wouldn't leave us…" she muttered out of earshot of Pierre. Sleep was difficult for them as they contemplated their circumstance. Alone.

With a shake of her feathered head, Sophie tried to leave behind the memories of that heart-wrenching day. Yet, five years on, the absence of her family was impossible to forget. Meanwhile, Pierre's excitement about a Halloween party and a treasure hunt was becoming infectious, and Sophie couldn't deny the tingling thrill of adventure stirring in her heart. Still, contemplating the risk of this invitation to some crazy Halloween party and a yet unknown treasure. Living in the branches of Babu was easy, safe, but the answers she craved were not found while perched within his magical care. She knew she had to pursue those questions no matter where it led and her sometimes knucklehead brother to get answers.

Her mind was in a swirl—she couldn't stop thinking that each trip they took may be their last or the chance of getting answers about their family may be on the next journey. Finally, her mind made up, treasure or no treasure, "We… GO!" Sophie took a big gulp of air and felt a sudden sense of peace.

"YES!" Pierre squawked in agreement, dancing on his perch, his beaked head tilting from side to side. "We could find the treasure, and then off to the Halloween party! It'll be the best day ever!"

Ever the optimist, Pierre rarely considered the consequences of their decisions. It seemed his passion for adventure had grown since their first encounter with Babu's magic branches and their trip to a Château in France.

"All right," Sophie nodded, folding the map under her wing. "But we need to stick together. And we need to be brave."

As the two parrots began planning their daring adventure, a newfound enthusiasm washed over them. Their ordinary day in the forest was now filled with anticipation of the unknown. The Halloween party, the treasure hunt—it all promised a great adventure. Little did they realize, they were on the threshold of a thrilling odyssey, destined to impart the virtues of courage, their true purpose, and the unbreakable bond of brother and sister.

The Scarecrow and the Cryptic Map

Forgetting the heat while still in Babu's branches, Pierre, using his beak and talons, opened the distressed old parchment, —a treasure map with frayed edges and a scribbled 'X' marking someplace. "Oh, how thrilling!" Sophie chirped while hopping up and down.

There's got to be a 'journey branch' that leads to the treasure, Pierre thought, studying the intricate lines of the map. *But where?*

Babu, ever watching and listening, rustled his leaves. His whispering voice filled the air. "The branch you seek, hidden within my roots, calls for caution... so be careful, my dear ones, for treasure is often hidden for a reason." Babu paused; his voice now more serious. "It is because the treasure you chase is ancient and holds many secrets. Beware, for there are beings who masquerade as something they are not, and much danger follows them."

This warning, coupled with their anticipation, made the young parrots' hearts flutter. Yet, their adventurous spirit overruled the threat of danger.

Sophie and Pierre swooped down into Babu's gnarled roots, discovering a branch glowing so faint the two almost missed it, but without hesitation, hopped on. With a rush of wind and whispers, the two birds were gone.

Arriving first in the strange land the magical root had brought them, Sophie landed on the vine of a large pumpkin. Watching her brother enter beak first, square into the center of an old rotten pumpkin. With a dramatic sucking noise, he pulled his face out with a force that sent the bird sprawling onto his red tail feathers. Sophie watched and shook her head, laughing at the sticky bits of pumpkin plastered to his beak and feathers. Straightening himself, spitting out the little chunks, Pierre looked around and saw a field of dull orange pumpkins. The birds took flight once more and soon realized it was an enormous pumpkin field, bathed in the softening golden light of the afternoon sun.

On the farthest border of the vast field, the two observed a figure leaning in solitude against a rough-hewn pole. The curious parrots saw him dressed in old, frayed clothes, its form half-human, half-symbol—a dilapidated, ancient scarecrow. The primeval fabric of its button eyes bore a small glint, kind of like a playful wink, enticing any onlooker into its bewitching world.

"Why, hello there, feathered companions," the old scarecrow croaked, a note of laughter present in his raspy voice. "Might you need help with your search for hidden treasure?"

Sophie's eyes met Pierre's, both brimming with astonishment. Their beaks hung open, unable to speak. Having never had a conversation with a scarecrow, the two birds were a bit taken aback. Yet, a curious trust tugged at their hearts, drawing them toward the strange figure.

"AHHHH... are you... are you speaking to us?" Sophie stuttered, her voice near a whisper. She exchanged a cautious glance with Pierre, her eyebrows arched in curiosity.

"Indeed, I am, Sophie," the scarecrow answered, the corners of his stitched smile seeming to rise. His voice

rustled like leaves scraping across a cobblestone street, calming in its familiarity. Sophie staggered backward, tripping over a vine.

"But how—" Pierre began, his voice trailing off, the scarecrow completing his question.

"—do I know your names? Let's say, the wind whispers many secrets."

There was a crafty quality to the old scarecrow, a wisdom that resided in the depths of his button eyes. The parrots felt a certain warmth coming from him—an unexpected kindness that pushed away their worries. They decided to cast aside their doubts for the moment, though Pierre with all his prior enthusiasm, held on to a bit of uncertainty. There was something that seemed wrong to the surprised bird. Then, he remembered his parents teaching him, *"making new friends, even in the most surprising corners of their world, was part of life's extraordinary journey."* He kept his thoughts to himself, not wanting to frighten Sophie with his first wary impression of the scarecrow.

Gathering her courage, Sophie asked, "Mr. Scarecrow, can you help us with our treasure hunt?"

A gust of wind blew across the field at that moment, causing the scarecrow to sway as though he were nodding.

Holding up a dusty hand, he pointed his bent finger to the sky. "Discovery! Exploration! Those are the essences of life! Of course, my dear," he chuckled as he untied himself from his rugged pole, his raspy laughter floating around them like the rustle of dry fallen leaves.

Together, with the wise scarecrow as their newfound guide, Sophie and Pierre stepped forward into the vast unknown. Their hearts pounded in their chests, not with fear, but exhilaration—a thrilling masterpiece of courage, growing trust, and the sweet promise of an extraordinary adventure.

The Whispering Woods

The glowing orb of the sun dipped low on the horizon, casting long, spooky shadows over the landscape near the edge of the pumpkin field. Sophie, Pierre, and the scarecrow stood at the threshold of a dense forest. A winding dirt path leading them deeper into the woods beckoned, following the gentle babble of a small stream somewhere in the distance.

The map, a collection of mysterious symbols and winding trails, pointed them toward the heart of the woods. As they ventured further, the din of the forest grew louder—the swooshing leaves, noisy unseen creatures, and haunting whispers adding layers of mystery to their quest. They were beginning to understand why it was called the "whispering woods".

"Into the woods we go!" Sophie proclaimed, her voice echoing amidst the strange whispers and eerie shadows. Her feathers ruffled in the cool evening breeze, the thrill of the adventure making her heart flutter.

The trio's entrance into the forest came with a sudden hush, followed by a creepy chorus of murmurs. It felt as though the woods had been awaiting their arrival, ready to share its long-held secrets. Some more treacherous than others.

"Listen," Pierre whispered, holding his wing out for silence. His eyes, wide with a mix of concern and excitement, darted around the forest.

Each whisper that floated on the wind was different—some sounded like a soft lullaby, others like a cryptic riddle, and a few like a chilling warning. Yet, beneath their frightening guise was an undercurrent of guidance.

"Listen, indeed," said the scarecrow, his raspy voice was quite calming amidst the eerie mutters. "These whispers are not to frighten but to guide us. Courage, young ones. Every adventurer's path has its share of shadows."

As the sun completely disappeared, the forest fell into a blanket of darkness, the only light coming from the Autumn moon's golden glow peeking through the towering canopy above. The dirt path, illuminated by the moonlight, became a line of silver cutting through the blackened woods. Both Sophie and Pierre could smell the pleasing night-time fragrance of sleeping flowers, mingled with the sturdy aroma of aged oak trees and the musk of old bark and soil that covered the winding path.

Each swirl of leaves, each mysterious whisper seemed louder and more profound in the night's silence. The crickets and toads sang their nightly chorus and added to each strange noise. Pierre listened and noticed that together the sounds took the shape of a riddle, a clue leading them closer to the treasure. He wondered, *what is this treasure we're so excited to find?* He began to have more doubts about the treasure, the scarecrow, and this dark forest, but he kept them to himself.

It's like the woods are showing us the path," Sophie whispered.

"Exactly, Sophie!" The scarecrow's approving chuckle echoed through the trees, bringing a small amount of warmth to the chilly night. "You are brave adventurers; the forest recognizes that spirit." Pierre knew it a little about bravery, but this was a new level of concern for him.

The path before them was restless with challenges and curiosities—unexpected bursts of rustling, whispered secrets that could not be deciphered, and the constant test of their daring to keep moving forward.

As they trudged deeper into the woods, the forest's voices—at first frightful—transformed into a comforting hum. Every whisper a reassurance, every crunch a subtle nudge in the right direction. That comfort provided Sophie a casual sense of safety. Unseen by the trio, a shadow knelt behind a tree, watching with curiosity as it moved like quiet a church mouse in the shadows, keeping an eye on the strange visitors.

As the moon rose higher, the mysterious whispering woods turned from an ominous foe to a trusted friend. The scarecrow's reminders of their bravery and adventurous spirit, coupled with the woods' puzzling murmurs, spurred Sophie and Pierre onward.

"The treasure waits for us, my friends," the scarecrow encouraged. "Into the heart of the whispering woods, under the watchful eyes of the moon. That's where our adventure leads."

Beneath the covering of the trees, the watchful gaze of the moon, and the mysterious shape in the shadows, Sophie and Pierre followed the scarecrow into the great unknown. The excitement of their quest hummed in the air around them, and the promise of the hidden treasure urged them on, deeper into the hypnotic woods.

The Pumpkin Graveyard

The trio continued deeper into the secretive forest still veiled in darkness. The yet unnamed scarecrow seemed to be growing more and more mysterious as they moved along the earthen path. His subtle side glances at the map and continued comments about "us" finding the treasure, he seemed almost too friendly. Sophie was deep in thought, almost trance-like when the scarecrow stopped without warning and held up his scratchy straw hand. Not seeing the unusual creature leading them, she stumbled into Pierre. "Uhgu-ufff-oh!" Jolted out of her daze, she said, "What is……?" Noticing the scarecrow's raised hand and his call for silence, Sophie fell quiet, her heart pounding in her small feathery chest. She shared a look of alarm with Pierre, both sets of parrot eyes reflecting the uneasiness they felt.

"Listen," the scarecrow whispered, his voice as soft as a swirling leaf. The woods had become quiet, the strange whispers lowered to a faint hum, almost as if the forest was holding its breath.

For a moment, the only sound was the gentle babble of the stream beside their path. It then began, a rhythmic rustling broke through the silence—growing louder. It seemed they were not alone in their quest; an unseen shadowy figure was trailing them, merging and emerging within the dark tangle of the woods.

"Sophie, Pierre," the scarecrow said, his voice quiet yet firm. "We are not alone. Our quest has gained the attention of someone… or something."

The parrots exchanged glances, their eyes wide with fear and intrigue. Sophie gulped. "Is it… is it a threat?"

"We do not know yet," the scarecrow replied. "But remember, courage is not the absence of fear, but the victory over it."

A sudden gust of swirling wind from behind them had them huddled closer. The mysterious creature was closing in, its presence blanketing them with a wave of uncertainty and uneasiness.

Their heartbeats echoed in their ears, their feathers stood on end, and the chill of fear touched their hearts. But they were not going to back down, not after coming so far. Determination hardened their gaze. Their spirits renewed with a fierce resolve—they would face whatever was trailing them, prepared for the trials that lay ahead.

"We will face this together," Pierre said, his voice steely, breaking the silence. Sophie nodded in agreement; her gaze fixed on the shadowy path ahead.

As they pressed onward, the unknown being's presence looming in the backdrop, the air filled with a heightened sense of danger. The parrots had never felt this before and yet their spirits refused to let fear decide their actions. Emboldened by the scarecrow's wisdom and their courage, Sophie and Pierre ventured further, prepared to face the trials that the whispering woods had in store.

The hush of the woods was broken by a sinister murmur that seemed to come from the depths of the forest. "Do you… hear that?" Sophie asked, her voice quivering with apprehension, the light gray feathers of her crest standing on end.

The scarecrow guide, his button eyes glinting with a mystery yet revealed, held up a straw-filled hand, his now coarse voice a whisper. "Indeed, it appears we have definitely attracted some company and I have an inkling I know who it is."

"Company?" Pierre echoed, his vibrant scarlet feathers ruffling in fear. Before the scarecrow could respond, a sudden rush echoed louder, now from in front of them, snapping twigs, scattering stones, the strange soundtrack to a figure unseen but without question, somewhere out there.

"We must go! I fear that scoundrel Badger is near," the scarecrow urged, his voice usually as calming as a warm autumn breeze now mixed with an uncharacteristic determination. He began to lead the parrots at a quicker pace, his straw-filled form rustling in harmony with the frantic beats of their hearts.

Racing through the forest, the shadowy figure tracking their every move, winding through the labyrinthine grove of whispering trees. The oppressive darkness of the woods gave way to an unexpected clearing. Blinking in surprise, they found themselves on the edge of a disturbing landscape, an arena they hadn't anticipated.

It was a ghoulish sight, a field dotted with large, rotting pumpkins carved into faces of eerie delight, their grotesque smiles forever frozen in decay. They stood on the trunks of gnarled, ancient trees, serving as bizarre tombstones under the silvery moonlight.

"This... this is a pumpkin graveyard!" Sophie gasped, her voice echoing in the eerie silence of the open space.

"I've never seen anything like this..." Pierre stuttered, his eyes wide with a mix of fear and curiosity.

"This place... it's creepy, but at the same time, so cool!" Sophie ventured; her eyes wide with fascination as she peered at a particularly menacing pumpkin.

Pierre chuckled; his fear, at least for the moment, forgotten. "Only you would find delight in a place like this, Sophie!"

"But that's what makes an adventure, doesn't it?" the scarecrow added with a wise nod. "Facing the unknown with courage and curiosity."

The scarecrow, now more at home among the strange pumpkins, nodded. "Yes, this forest is a cauldron of many secrets. The Pumpkin Graveyard is one of them. But worry not; it may offer us relief from our pursuer."

As the scarecrow moved on, weaving his way through the maze of tombstones, the shadowy badger kept a keen eye on the two strangers. The badger thought to himself, *I have seen these two in the past.* He was familiar with crows and hawks, even the mysterious silent owl Luna, who on occasion would make a nightly appearance to show the badger and his clan she was keeping a watchful eye on the strange community. "But with these two," he whispered to himself, "this is going to demand a solid plan to get what rightfully belongs to me and my clan." He'd been waiting years. The lost map of Samhain and the bountiful treasure. He recalled the ancient Celtic ritual marking the end of a bountiful harvest, but never enjoyed the bounty the goddess Pomona promised. The badger continued, hidden in the shadows, his steely dark eyes never leaving the two strangers.

Bathed in the glow of the moon, the Pumpkin Graveyard looked unnatural, yet captivating. Each pumpkin, with its ghastly grin, seemed to have a tale etched on its decaying face. In this coldhearted landscape, Sophie and Pierre found themselves drawn into a tale spun from threads of history and myth.

Clasped tight in Sophie's talons was the weathered map, a parchment bearing cryptic symbols and marks, a beacon guiding them toward a lost treasure buried in time. As they moved on, Sophie thought to herself, *I wonder why the scarecrow is so interested in this map. Why does he keep looking at it?* She realized with the scarecrow's strange actions and something following them, *this is no ordinary map.*

The Scarecrow's Tale of Samhain and the Goddess Pomona

Under the watchful gaze of the ancient, grinning pumpkin tombstones, Sophie and Pierre nestled closer to the scarecrow. The cool night air whirled the leaves overhead, creating a soothing melody that only underscored their growing anticipation. The scarecrow began to tell a tale of the ancient past, trance-like as he began, the two young birds felt as though they were in a dream.

"The tale of the map you embrace," began the scarecrow, his straw-filled hand giving a gentle touch to the parchment in Sophie's grip, "begins long, long ago in the northern islands, where the winds are chilling and fierce."

He paused, letting the silence of the pumpkin graveyard seep into his tale, his voice becoming hollow and other worldly—his eyes seemingly glazing over with the past speaking through his words. "In these lands, there thrived Celtic tribes, brave and spiritual. Every year, as the bountiful summer gave way to the stark winter, they celebrated Samhain, a festival of mystery and reverence where the living could reach out to those beyond the grave. There was a celebration of Pomona, the sacred goddess of fruits and trees, and whose symbol was the apple."

With his words, the parrots relived the memories of ancient celebrations. They were drawn into the echoes and rhythms and the subtle hints of spirits whispering joyful notes of Celtic chants.

"When the powerful Roman Empire absorbed the Celtic lands, their traditions blended, much like a stream joining a river," the scarecrow continued, his voice, feather-light and subtle, drifted through the air with delicate grace. "And so, the Celtic festival of Samhain found kinship with Feralia, a Roman day of remembering those who had passed. Both traditions held a common belief—honoring the dead. And it was on the sacred night of Samhain that this very map was born."

Sophie and Pierre held their breath as the scarecrow's story washed over them. Sophie's grip on the ancient map tightening. "They believed that the spirits, free to roam on Samhain night, guided their hands, revealing the secret location of a treasure so grand, it would ensure prosperity for their tribe."

"The Celts, in their wisdom, inked the spirits' guidance on this parchment, creating the map you now hold," the scarecrow concluded. "Only on the night of Samhain, when the spirits roam free again, can the treasure show itself to those who are worthy."

The silence that followed was only broken by the now voiceless wind. As Sophie and Pierre looked at the map anew, they felt the weight of its history, the whispers of its creation, and the secret it held. Their adventure was not only about finding the treasure, but it was also about respecting the ancient customs that had guided them to this moment.

As the three companions sat in the heart of the pumpkin graveyard, beneath the ancient, grinning tombstones, the tale of the map seemed to come alive in the flickering moonlight, adding a new chapter to their thrilling quest.

Now, the map, a remnant of ancient customs and changing times, had found its way into the possession of Sophie and Pierre. Yet, they were not the only ones interested in the map's secrets.

From the shadows of the Pumpkin Graveyard, the pair of keen eyes followed the parrots. A peculiar badger, known for his strange interest in historical artifacts, wanted the ancient map. He had followed the parrots from the whispering woods to the graveyard, hoping to relieve them of the map before too many found out about their presence in this land.

"Look, Pierre," Sophie said, her voice low, "we're not alone here. Do you see those eyes twinkling in the darkness?"

"I do," replied Pierre, his gaze fixed on the shadowy figure. "We have to be careful."

The scarecrow, standing tall amidst the pumpkin tombstones, nodded. "The treasure we seek is valuable, and its allure attracts more than our little band of adventurers. We must stay together and be alert."

They ventured deeper into the Pumpkin Graveyard; the badger's watchful gaze never left them. Unseen dangers lurked around every corner, and the treasure was still a mystery waiting to show itself to those who had proven themselves true and honorable. Through the strange customs of ancient times, the allure of a long-lost treasure, and the pursuit of a mysterious badger, Sophie and Pierre were realizing that their adventure was turning out to be more thrilling than they could have ever imagined.

As the trio explored further, it seemed as though the bulging eyes of the grotesque faces were watching every step as they slogged through the graveyard. Their journey had taken an unexpected detour, complete with shadowy pursuers and a graveyard of pumpkin tombstones. The whispering woods, their wise scarecrow guide, and their own unyielding resolve continued to test their spirit as they trekked deeper into the night. Little did they know, their greatest challenges and most fascinating discoveries were yet to come.

A Ghostly Gathering and Crooked Straw

ophie and Pierre had become accustomed to the strange sights and sounds, they had the unusual feeling they had been in this place before but couldn't remember when or where. They weren't sure where they were, but as they came around a sharp corner in the graveyard and stepped into the clearing, a riot of colors and noises greeted them. It was the grand Halloween party, a spectacular assembly of ghosts, ghouls, and other supernatural beings that lurked in the shadows. The large open field, covered in beaten down grass and ferns, was the perfect place for the spooky gathering that now unfolded before them.

Underneath the gleaming moonlight, they could see lively phantoms darting about, a group of goblins huddled around a bubbling cauldron, and a few werewolves engaged in a howling contest. There was a peculiar sense of merriment in the air—an enchanting blend of fear, excitement, and sheer shining joy. It was chaos, but a thrilling, enjoyable one.

"Pierre," Sophie whispered, trying not to stare too much at a ghoul munching on a candy bone. "Do you think they knew we were coming?"

"Seems like it," Pierre anxiously replied, eyeing a group of witches that waved at them from across the clearing. "I bet that sly badger spread the word about us."

And indeed, unbeknownst to the trio, the sly badger had engaged in a hushed conversation with a few unnerving creatures, glancing toward the birds from time to time.

But Sophie and Pierre refused being sidetracked, the awareness of their goal to find the treasure and whatever else lay before them was always on their mind. They spent the night navigating through the crowd of chattering monsters with nervous apprehension, making new allies, listening to stories from the wolves, and learning about the many secrets of the whispering woods and the pumpkin graveyard.

As the night grew deeper, they stumbled upon a group of friendly apparitions huddled around a bonfire. After some initial nervousness, they struck up a conversation, learning about the customs of the ethereal beings.

"It's all about adaptability, ain't it?" remarked one ghost, his transparent hand gesturing. "We all have our quirks, our peculiar habits, but we learn to live and let live."

Meanwhile, the scarecrow, with his unconventional charm, had become the life of the party. The forest folk, intrigued by his story, asked about his peculiar name. With a twinkle in his button eyes, the scarecrow spun his tale.

"Ah, the night I became Crooked Straw," he began, his button eyes reflecting the flickering bonfire light, casting dancing shadows around the curious crowd. "It was a night unlike any other, filled with an electricity that was more than the approaching storm. You see, without ceremony they placed me in a farmer's field, my purpose to scare away the crows who were pecking at the seeds my farmer had planted." He moved around the bonfire with a certain grace and flair, adding intrigue, seeming to draw his audience further into his tale. He paused; his gaze distant as he recalled that fateful night. "The skies were a deep, threatening gray, heavy with unshed rain. Thunder roared and rumbled in the distance like an angry beast. The air was alive with a sense of anticipation."

His audience, rapt in attention, could almost hear the distant thunderclaps, could almost smell the scent of damp earth and the impending rainfall.

"Then it happened," Crooked Straw continued. "BAM! A flash of lightning, bright and blinding, lanced down from the heavens. It struck me, tearing through my straw-filled body, warping and twisting my wooden frame into a bizarre, crooked form."

A gasp went up around the bonfire. The parrots, despite knowing the end of the story, found themselves leaning in, captivated by Crooked Straw's narration.

"But you know what?" Crooked Straw said, his voice dropping to a soft murmur. "That lightning, as much as it twisted me, it instilled in me something unique, something that set me apart from the other scarecrows. The bolt, instead of destroying me, gave me a sense of purpose," he smiled, touching his crooked form. "And so, when the storm passed and the sun rose on a new day, I found myself standing taller despite my twisted structure. I was no longer a plain scarecrow. I was Crooked Straw, named after what could have been my downfall became my strength, my defining trait."

"Instead of allowing the event to make me feel broken or less, I embraced my new form, my new name, and my new resolve. I learned that it's our uniqueness that sets us apart, and that there is a higher power that gives us our identity. And that, my friends," he finished, a profound calmness washing over his face, "is how Crooked Straw was born."

His tale ended in a blanket of silence before applause and cheers erupted from his captivated audience. The tale of Crooked Straw, a new purpose of resilience and tolerance, of embracing one's differences, had touched them all, inspiring the listeners under the Halloween moonlight. He thought, *I have begun to collect my followers—how easy to manipulate them.* As the badger watched and listened from a distance, he set about making a plan to retrieve what is rightfully his. The map to the treasure of Samhain.

As the sun began to creep into the sky, the trio left the party, a little wiser, a little braver, and with a few more friends in their corner. The Halloween gathering had been a unique experience, one that would always remain etched in their memories. Unbeknownst to them, their journey was about to take a twist, but for now, they reveled in the joy of the night that had passed.

A Conflict Within

Half asleep as they worked their way to the next point on the map, Crooked Straw recommended they find a safe spot to rest. All the weary birds could muster was a weary squawk as sleep overtook them both.

Their feathered heads tucked neatly toward their back, Crooked Straw—not requiring rest as quiet as his scratchy body would allow—crept over to the sleeping birds and slid the tattered map from Sophie's now relaxed talons. Moving around the backside of the large oak tree, Crooked Straw opened the old worn document. His eyes grew wide as he let out an uncomfortable groan.

Realizing where they must go to recover the hidden treasure, his barn straw-filled head needed a plan, and he needed it now. He had known of rumors of the Samhain treasure but never thought them to be more than a tall tale. Yet, when he saw the age-old mark of the goddess Pomona, still encrusted with flecks of the most ancient gold leaf known, he realized his two feathered friends were here for more than only finding hidden treasure. They had a much more significant purpose. The entire mystery surrounding where they were from and how they arrived began to make a bit more sense as he scanned the ragged old document.

Realizing his importance in the journey, Crooked Straw understood the hard decisions he'd have to make for the two exceptional birds to discover the sought-after treasure. Only then could the kingdom reclaim its past splendor and purge it from the darkness that had ruled for so many years. The stormy night from ages ago that bent his frame had also left him nearly devoid of emotions. He knew his soul and spirit and been compromised that night. Still, a few feelings crept into the straw figure, and strangely, he found he had grown attached to the duo.

Crooked Straw shook his hay-stuffed noggin and pushed down any indication of having feelings for the two birds. He must focus on his sole purpose for guiding them to that Samhain prize he needed. He knew that failure would lead to the pair forever remaining captive in this strange world he called home. The darkness held an evil power over the land and was capable of holding intruders in shadowy cages. Sophie and Pierre assumed they were on a fun adventure to find treasure, and then off to a Halloween party. For now, he would keep the truth from the eager pair. They'd soon recognize their true role in the treasure hunt and why they arrived with the map.

With the pair still deep in sleep, he stared at the tattered document in an attempt to recall any symbols his straw brain could understand. It would help him decide the best course of action. *There are too many clues I can't interpret*, he thought to himself. Though he now knew the treasure was real and not tales and rumors told around the campfire. Despite his physical limitations, he would somehow find a way to claim it and restore the realm to its former glory.

Unfortunately, like a cloud that appears on the horizon and then disappears, new thoughts the straw man had didn't stay long enough in his head for a clear idea of what he was to do. He could tell tales from the past and spin great stories of former rulers and mysterious events, but he struggled to form fresh ideas. It was his solitary flaw. It was a passing moment when he had clear thinking and then disappear as quick as it came. As these deliberations and the seeming confusion continued, they created a good amount of conflict for the scratchy old creature. He knew he couldn't deny his fondness for the two feathered strangers no matter what the lightening did to his body and his soul that night.

No sooner did that realization come to him, another more sinister idea developed. It arose from deep inside and quickly had a strong hold on him. He could finally fulfill his destiny, the destiny he deserved, and when these two strange birds landed in *HIS* field, it started.

They will help me find and recover this ancient treasure. It's a sign, me, Crooked Straw, will rule this kingdom, he thought to himself raising a dusty bent hand. "The badger and his clan of rebels will indeed know the power of Crooked Straw. And with the blessing of the goddess Pomona, ordained as rightful ruler." At first, he found himself whispering his thoughts but was now speaking as if in a trance to the entire forest around them. His voice slowly growing in intensity as his raspy decree was proclaimed, "It was HE who stood guard over the crops of this fertile estate." He pounded on his bent chest. "It was HE who saw all that came and left from this strange land."

Crooked Straw went on with his scheming plans, eager to convince the two birds they were on an adventure to find a few trinkets, have a nice party, then return from where they came.

The Betrayal and a Badger

In the light of the early dawn Sophie's eyes fluttered open, the incredible memories of the Halloween celebration swirled around in her mind. The clearing, once filled with laughter and dancing during the Halloween celebration was now quiet. The ghosts and ghouls had vanished with the night, leaving only a soft rustling of leaves to welcome the new day.

Turning to embrace the morning, she looked up and took in a scene she hadn't expected. She spotted Crooked Straw hunched over something; his usually jolly demeanor replaced by an intense focus. As her vision sharpened, a sinking feeling settled in her stomach. He was studying their treasure map, the very one she had thought was safe.

Crooked Straw looked up, his eyes widening as he saw her watching. He gave her a broad, straw-filled smile that didn't quite reach his eyes. "Good morning, young, feathered friend! I was just... admiring the artistry of this old map you had. The symbols and markings are quite perplexing, don't you think?"

Sophie's instincts told her something was amiss. Her heart pounded as she nudged Pierre awake, her eyes never leaving Crooked Straw's face. "Pierre, wake up. Something's not right."

"What's going on?" Pierre mumbled, rubbing his eyes, but seeing the situation understood. He rocketed into the air and zoomed straight at Crooked Straw's face, his wings a blur of color.

Crooked Straw stumbled back in surprise, losing his grip on the map. Sophie seized the moment and darted forward, snatching the map from his grasp. But it tore in two, with both Sophie and Crooked Straw holding a crucial piece.

The birds shot up to the safety of a tall tree while Crooked Straw called out after them, his voice filled with a mix of frustration and desperation.

"Wait, please! Let me explain!" he shouted, his voice cracking. "I never meant to deceive you. I was only trying to understand the clues better."

Sophie and Pierre looked at each other, their hearts pounding. They glanced down at Crooked Straw's earnest face but decided to keep flying.

As they flew over the mysterious land, their minds were a whirlwind of emotions. Why had he taken the map? Why had they trusted him after they arrived? Where was he leading them? The thrill of the treasure hunt had taken a turn, and now was faced with uncertainty and betrayal. They had never known these suspicions and weren't sure how to express their thoughts, so they flew on.

Not sure where to go or what to do next, the sight of an apple orchard and a sunflower garden filled their vision. Realizing how hungry they were, they descended to eat. Lost in discussion about a plan and what to do next, a haunting hoot filled the air.

A wise old owl named Luna appeared, landing on a nearby branch, her eyes deep and knowing. The parrots, frightened and not knowing who or what to trust, stared at the large old bird with apprehension. Was this bird real or another ghost? Luna's gentle voice soon calmed them as she looked into the birds' eyes, reflecting the trust in her soul.

"My dear young ones," she said, her soothing voice, filled with ancient wisdom. "I know of your quest, and I see the burden you bear and for more than treasure. Trust in what you know to be right, but also be mindful of others. Not all things are as they seem. Sometimes, the most twisted paths lead to the brightest treasures."

With those cryptic words, Luna took to the sky, leaving Sophie and Pierre to ponder her wisdom.

They feasted on juicy apples and sunflower seeds, considering Luna's words. It was clear that they were part of something bigger than a treasure hunt. There were secrets yet to uncover, and they would need to trust not only themselves but find an ally to confide in as well.

As they nibbled on their meal, both Sophie and Pierre began to see Crooked Straw in a new light. Was he taking advantage of them, or was he too caught up in the excitement of the treasure hunt? Had his own fears and desires clouded his judgment? The idea that even Crooked Straw could make mistakes made him seem more real, more alive, despite his straw-filled frame.

It was then that Pierre told Sophie of his apprehension about Crooked Straw, that he seemed a little too eager to help us when we first met near the whispering woods. "I don't know, Sophie, maybe that faceplant into the pumpkin knocked something loose in my brain. It just made me a little weary of him." "Why didn't you tell me before this all started?" Sophie inquired, not angry but a little confused.

"I didn't want to frighten you. I may be your younger brother, but I am your protector, too," Pierre replied, though a bit sheepishly. Sophie's eyes softened, her love for her brother growing yet again.

Pierre looked at Sophie, his eyes filled with determination. "Whatever happens, we'll face it together."

Sophie nodded, her heart swelling with love and pride for her brave brother. They were in this adventure together, and come what may, they'd find their way through it.

Discussing their next move, they opened the map, though almost half of it gone now and in the hands of Crooked Straw. What they saw surprised them. Gazing upon the strange markings and cryptic shapes that adorned it, they realized they possessed clues of its exact hidden whereabouts in the secret chamber. It was buried in the depths of an old, abandoned mansion. Their part of the map also depicted how to navigate the dilapidated old castle. What they lacked were the directions to its location.

Still determined, Sophie and Pierre flew onward, the excitement of the treasure hunt now tinged with the uncertainty of betrayal. Thoughts of Crooked Straw's actions weighed on their minds. They had trusted him, welcomed him into their adventure, and now they felt the sting of his deception. But as they soared above the landscape, a nagging question remained: What was the true purpose of their quest? The torn map was a symbol of their fractured understanding, and they knew they had only scratched the surface of a deeper mystery.

But they couldn't dwell on that for long, for a new figure caught their attention. From below, a badger was waving at them, his eyes full of urgency. They exchanged glances, both feeling a sense of apprehension but also curiosity.

The badger seemed to sense their hesitation, his voice carrying on the wind, "Please, hear me out! I have information about the treasure, about the map! I mean you no harm!"

Sophie and Pierre circled above, still wary, but something in the badger's eyes spoke of sincerity. They finally decided to descend to the treetops, keeping a safe distance, their eyes sharp and attentive.

The badger introduced himself as Archibald and began to unravel a tale that was both fascinating and perplexing. He spoke of an abandoned mansion, of a hidden treasure, and of a history intertwined with the map they held.

"I am the last heir of the realm according to the map," Archibald explained, his voice filled with emotion. "The mansion holds the secrets of our land, the wisdom of ages past, and the key to restoring the balance long lost."

He spoke of a time when life flowed without a hint of danger, when creatures of all kinds lived in harmony, and when the mansion was a beacon of knowledge and enlightenment. But something had changed, a dark shadow had fallen, and the mansion had become a place of mystery and fear.

"The map you hold is more than a path to treasure," Archibald continued, his voice trembling with passion. "It's a key to our past, a guide to our future, and a symbol of hope for all the creatures of our kingdom."

He looked at Sophie and Pierre with earnest eyes. "I do not know the exact location of the mansion, nor do I know how to retrieve the treasure. But together, we can uncover the secrets that—" he paused, caught up with his deep emotion and trembling, trying to finish. "—that for generations—" he still stumbled on his word, "—were hidden from us." Gathering himself, quietly considering that these two strange creatures are what was foretold in the ancient scrolls to bring their land back to greatness, "We can bring light to the darkness and restore the glory of our land."

His words, filled with a sense of urgency and desperation, a plea for trust and collaboration. Sophie and Pierre felt a connection to his story, a sense of purpose that went beyond their simple quest for treasure.

But they also felt a nagging doubt, a lingering suspicion that kept them from embracing Archibald's tale. They were deceived once before, and they couldn't shake the feeling that there was more to this story than met the eye.

"We need time to think," Pierre finally said, his voice firm but thoughtful. "Your story is compelling, but we must be cautious. Someone misled us before, and we need to be sure of our path moving forward."

Archibald nodded; his face filled with understanding. "I will wait here, ready to assist you whenever you decide. The fate of our realm depends on us, and I know that together we can achieve great things."

With a mixture of hope and trepidation, Sophie and Pierre took to the sky once more, leaving Archibald behind. They soared above the landscape, their minds a whirlwind of thoughts and emotions.

Was he telling the truth? Could they trust him? Were they part of a grander quest, a journey that held the key to a realm's redemption?

The questions swirled around them, adding a layer of complexity to their adventure, a twist of perplexity that both excited and bewildered them. They felt the thrill of the unknown, the rush of discovery, and the pull of a destiny that seemed to be calling them forward.

But they also felt the weight of responsibility, the burden of trust, and the challenge of navigating a path filled with twists and turns. The map they held was more than a simple guide; it was a symbol of their connection to something greater, to something very personal, it was a link to a past that was waiting for the right time to uncover the truth.

The torn map was like a puzzle, a riddle that held the secrets of their quest. It was a reminder of the fragility of trust and the complexity of their journey. And it was a challenge, a call to adventure that would test their courage, their wisdom, and their faith in each other.

The Vex Shadows and a Trail of Trust

Sophie and Pierre, perched high on a towering oak, exchanged nervous glances. Both deep in their own thoughts, weighed their options for achieving the goal of the treasure and whatever it held. The treetops swayed in the gentle breeze below them, masking the ground and the badger, who waited with hope in his eyes.

Pierre's voice broke the tense silence, "We don't have many options. The path to the treasure seems blocked at every turn, and if there's even a chance Archibald is genuine, shouldn't we take it? Can we trust him?"

"Can we trust him?" Sophie thought to herself, she hesitated, the memories of Crooked Straw's betrayal still fresh in her mind. *"Can we trust him?"* She asked herself again, pausing for a long moment lost in thought. Sophie was a kind and gentle spirit but devastated by the deception played on them. She put on a strong face ever since their family went missing so long ago. Sophie hid this painful memory from Pierre, she thought she needed to be strong for him. But all that had happened

the past few days showed that her little brother was stronger than he let on. Once again, she shook off those thoughts and continued.

Sophie sighed. "I don't know. I think that's the point—to trust, even when it's hard."

Making their decision, they descended to meet Archibald. The badger's eyes shone with gratitude. "Thank you," he said simply.

And so, with a leap of faith, their partnership began.

The first test of trust came sooner than expected. A few days into their journey, while searching for clues, they encountered their first test. Deep in the whispering woods, sinister beings were watching, waiting to destroy and take from the trio their very spirit to carry on.

These nefarious creatures thrived in darkness, wanting nothing more than to maintain the realm's shadowy status quo. At their leader's command, the Vex Shadows would move in on the trio, their whispery forms twisting and turning like smoke. Their goal was to separate and disorient.

The Vex Shadows were not creatures but manifestations of the darkness that had enveloped the realm. Their existence was a chilling reminder of what the land had become, twisted and corrupted. The essence of the shadows was woven into the fabric of the Vex Shadows, making them elusive, deceptive, and treacherous.

The Vex Shadows were devoid of any physical form, appearing as whispery figures that could be mistaken for fog or a trick of the eye. Their presence was often accompanied by a sudden drop in temperature, and their eyes—the only discernible feature—glowed with a wicked red light.

They moved with a sinister grace, their bodies twisting and turning, always changing shape. At times, they resembled dark, writhing vines; at other moments, they took on more humanoid forms, their faces contorted into grotesque expressions.

Their voice, when they chose to speak, was a hollow echo, a sound that seemed to come from everywhere and nowhere all at once. It was a voice that sent chills down the spine and left an unsettling feeling long after it had faded.

The leader of the Vex Shadows, known as Shade, a being of concentrated darkness and malice. Shade's control over the shadows was absolute, and its commands

carried out without question. Unlike its followers, Shade had a more defined form, a silhouette of pure darkness.

They operated under a strict order, with Shade at the top and his underlings executing Shade's will with precision.

There was singular purpose: to maintain the realm's shadowy status quo. They thrived in darkness and feared the return of light, for light would mean their destruction. The treasure of Samhain represented a threat to their existence, a power that could dispel the shadows and bring balance back to the realm.

Their tactics were cruel and calculated. They sought to separate and disorient their victims, attacking not only physically but mentally as well. They were masters of illusion, able to create visions of one's deepest fears, turning allies against each other and spreading conflict.

When they moved in on Sophie, Pierre, and Archibald, it was with this intent. They isolated Pierre, using illusions to make him see Sophie and Archibald as enemies. At the same time, they attacked Sophie and Archibald's minds, attempting to break their will and trust in one another.

Their whispers were laden with deceit, promising power, wealth, and safety in exchange for abandoning the quest. They knew the animal psyche, playing on doubts and fears, making their victims question everything they knew and believed.

In the ensuing chaos, cornered by a cast of shadowy beings closing in, Pierre heard an ear rattling battle cry that echoed off the trees. A group of badgers emerged from the thicket, led by none other than Archibald's sister, Aurelian. Their fierce and united front drove the Vex Shadows away, proving Archibald's trustworthiness and the strength of his clan.

After the skirmish, a shaken Pierre confessed, "I was scared... I felt so alone." Sophie placed a comforting wing on his shoulder.

"Remember, no matter how dark the path, there's always a light. Today, that light was Archibald and his clan."

They learned from the badger the Vex Shadows had one critical weakness: they were creatures of darkness and thus vulnerable to light. In their confrontation with the trio, the unexpected arrival of Archibald's clan, united and strong, created a symbolic beacon of light, their love and trust for one another acting as a shield against the Vex Shadows' sinister influence.

Their journey, it seemed, was tense with danger at every stage. Yet, with each challenge, they grew stronger, understanding that their strength was in unity.

Pierre, finding inspiration from their victories, began to stand taller, his voice more assertive. He became a force to reckon with, not only defending against attackers but also taking charge in challenging situations. The timid young bird had transformed into a fearless leader.

The evening of the third day in this mystical land, each animal from the badger clan to the parrots fell exhausted from travel and always on the lookout for the next challenge to their quest. Sophie, while deciphering a coded message from the torn map, demonstrated her intellect again. A series of riddles that seemed impossible to decipher, but either a hunch or intuition led her to locate a concealed cave where the next clue lay hidden. As her droopy eyes faded, she clutched the sacred document firmly in her talons. It could wait until tomorrow.

The Hidden Chamber of Time

Sophie's eyes sparkled with curiosity as they approached the hidden cave. The entrance, obscured by overhanging vines, promised secrets yet uncovered. Her heart quickened. Something was calling to her.

"Quite the find, I must say," Archibald commented, his nose twitching with interest. "What's hiding in there?"

Pierre glanced at his sister, noting the intense look in her eyes. "Sophie, you've got that look again. What's going on in that head of yours?"

Sophie hesitated before answering, her voice soft. "Pierre, it's like... like the cave is whispering to me."

They ventured into the cave, the temperature dropping as they went deeper. The walls, adorned with strange markings unlike anything they had ever seen.

The cave was more than a dark, hidden recess in the landscape; it was an ancient place, a storehouse of memories and wisdom that reached back through the eons. As Sophie, Pierre, and Archibald ventured deeper, they were immediately struck by the cave's atmosphere, a blend of mystery and reverence that seemed to permeate everything.

The smell was the first thing that caught their attention. A rich, earthy scent filled the air, mingling with the faint aroma of aged parchment and dried herbs. It was the smell of time itself, of centuries buried and preserved, waiting for the curious to uncover its secrets.

As they walked, their footsteps echoed through the dimly lit chambers. Shadows clung to the rough-hewn walls, hiding in crevices and darting across the floor as Archibald's torch flickered and danced. Stalactites hung from the ceiling like ancient guardians, glistening with moisture while their counterparts, the stalagmites, reached upward like the hands of the forgotten reaching for the present.

The cave was not lacking life. Small insects buzzed in hidden corners, and the occasional rustle of unseen creatures added to the cave's mysterious charm. Moss and lichen adorned some of the rocks, their soft green providing a subtle contrast to the brown and gray shades of the stone.

But what mesmerized the trio was the intricate artistry etched into the walls. Scenes of harvest, dance, and family gatherings told stories of a civilization connected to the land and each other. Symbols and motifs, interwoven with depictions of celestial bodies, hinted at a profound understanding of time's cyclical nature.

Touching the walls, Sophie could feel the rough texture of the stone, cold to the touch but somehow infused with warmth from the hands that had carved them. Pierre found himself drawn to the rhythmic sound of dripping water, a timeless beat that seemed to connect with his soul.

Archibald's keen badger senses were particularly attuned to the cave's ambiance. He noted the way the air felt thick with history, almost touchable. He joked about the cave's "musty charm," but even he couldn't deny the profound sense of connection he felt with the place.

The cave was a living testament to a way of life that had long since vanished, a haunting yet beautiful reminder of a past not forgotten. It was a place where time seemed to stand still, allowing them to reach out and touch a world that once was.

As they explored further, they found themselves wrapped in a cloak of awe. They were mere visitors in a place that had seen the rise and fall of a civilization, a place that held secrets, wisdom, and the whispering echoes of a time long past. The dark old cave had welcomed them, embraced them, and, for a fleeting moment, had allowed them to become part of something far greater than themselves.

Sophie reached out to touch one, her wing trembling. It was a strange disc, with symbols radiating outwards, interwoven with depictions of the sun, moon, and stars. "It's beautiful," she whispered.

Archibald scratched his head in bewilderment.

Pierre, drawn to another device, a set of interconnected rings that seemed to rotate and align in a puzzling pattern. "Look at this! It's like they were measuring time in a completely different way."

They explored further, finding a small passageway that led to an unseen chamber. Inside, the air seemed to hum with ancient insight, filled with artifacts, scrolls, and intricate carvings that spoke of a civilization that once thrived.

Examining the room, they began to understand. This culture valued the land, treating it with reverence, seeing time not as a relentless march but as a dance of seasons. They celebrated family, connecting generations through stories and traditions.

Sophie's eyes filled with wonder. "They saw time as a circle, a continuous loop connecting everything. Past, present, future—all one."

They interacted with some of the enchanted pieces, each one a riddle, each riddle a step closer to the next clue in their quest. As they puzzled over the ancient artifacts, they began to see the riddle on the map in a new light.

"Look!" Pierre exclaimed, pointing at the manuscript. "These symbols match the ones on the map! It's telling us something."

Sophie's intuition began to piece it together. "The treasure of Samhain isn't about riches. It's about understanding, connecting, honoring what came before. These citizens valued patience, family, respect, and their connection with the land."

Archibald nodded, his face serious. "A lesson for us all. The real treasure is the wisdom they left behind."

They continued to explore, each discovery a burst of understanding, each moment a connection to a past that was neither gone nor forgotten. They learned about the creature's rituals, their way of life, their deep understanding of nature's rhythms.

As they left the cave, a sense of awe settled over them. They had not only found another clue to their treasure but also uncovered a legacy, a glimpse into a world where time was not an enemy but a friend.

Archibald's voice broke the silence. "You know, it's funny. We spend our lives chasing time. Perhaps it's time we learned to dance with it instead."

Sophie smiled, squeezing her brother's wing. "The treasure we seek isn't only gold and jewels, but the wisdom to live in harmony with time and each other."

The three of them looked back at the cave, the hidden chamber now a part of them, guiding them on their journey, not just towards treasure but towards understanding. They had learned valuable lessons about patience, history, and time's fleeting nature.

With a newfound sense of purpose, they continued on their quest, the cave's whispers still echoing in their hearts, promising that the path they were on was not an adventure but a journey of discovery, connection, and wisdom.

The Badger's Birthright

The rays of the setting sun danced through the leaves as the trio left the secret cavern behind. The warmth and beauty of the forest contrasted hard with the urgency settling over them.

"Archibald," Sophie asked, her voice tinged with both excitement and concern, "what was the meaning of the golden seal on the map? It seems to resonate with something very deep in the history of this land."

The badger's eyes twinkled, and he began to speak, his voice reverberating with a sense of gravity. "Ah, Sophie, you have a keen eye indeed. That golden seal is the inauguration of my ancestors, bestowed by the goddess Pomona herself. Let me tell you a tale of old."

The trio continued their journey as Archibald unraveled the story, weaving through dense foliage and narrow paths. The forest seemed to listen, and the very earth beneath them felt alive with the weight of history.

"Centuries ago," Archibald began, pausing to clear his throat, "badgers served as guardians of the realm. Anointed if you will. We defended the cold northern isles from marauding creatures pursuing the treasure we now seek."

"The Vex Shadows?" Pierre asked, his feathers ruffled with unease.

"Yes, the very same, and others, but none as evil as the Vex," Archibald replied, his tone serious. "A dark force that threatens to consume all that is good in our land.

The treasure we seek has the power to free us from their grasp. My clan lived in peace and fellowship for centuries until they arrived."

Sophie's mind whirred with questions, she finally asked, "how did your clan become the guardians? What makes the badgers special?"

Archibald's eyes glinted with ancestral pride. "Chosen for our courage, wisdom, and loyalty. The etchings in the cave, placed there as historical proof of our rightful rule. Until today, I'd only heard stories, but seeing them with my own eyes has renewed my faith in our cause."

The journey was difficult, the sun had now settled low in the sky. The trio found themselves in a clearing, surrounded by ancient trees and moss-covered rocks. The whispers of leaves and the distant calls of unseen creatures were the only sounds as they decided to rest.

Sophie, her mind still filled with the rich history Archibald had shared, found a mossy rock to sit on while Pierre perched himself on a low-hanging branch. Archibald, never at rest, continued to prowl the area, sniffing at the earth and inspecting the undergrowth.

As they were about to dig into some provisions, Sophie's eye caught a glint of something unusual. A beam of sunlight had found its way through the dense foliage, illuminating a small patch of ground near an ancient oak tree. The light was reflecting off something half-buried in the earth.

"What's that over there?" Sophie squinted, pointing towards the strange gleam.

Archibald's ears perked up. He followed Sophie's gaze. They approached the spot, curiosity growing with each step. The sunlight continued to dance on the object, as if inviting them closer. Sophie reached down and brushed away the leaves and dirt, revealing a metallic surface, decorated but tarnished by time.

"This looks old," she whispered, her feathered wing tracing the ornate patterns.

Pierre fluttered down from his perch, his bright eyes wide with interest. "It's beautiful! But what is it?"

Archibald's nose twitched as he examined the artifact. "This is no ordinary object. This is a relic from the civilization we learned about in the cave. See these markings? They match the etchings we saw."

Archibald, with care, unearthed the artifact, holding it up to the light. The sunlight seemed to play with it creating mesmerizing reflections. It was a key, its handle shaped like a coiled serpent its eyes set with glittering stones.

"A key," Archibald voiced, awe in his voice. "Could this be the key to the treasure?" Deep in thought and mumbling to himself, he said, "If this is the key, then we, I have been entrusted to fulfill that which was prophesied ages ago." Realizing he had been talking to himself, he came back out of his thoughts and said, "This key has been lost for ages. Many have sought this relic as it opens the treasure that gives dominion over the realm."

His eyes took on a determined focus. Sought by many through the ages the sunlight had disclosed it to the trio for a reason, entrusting them with what had remained an unfulfilled quest for countless others. They all stared at the key, in their eyes a satisfying sense of purpose. It was a step forward in their pursuit, brought to them by a combination of chance and fate. The path was becoming clear, the connection to the land and its history deepening. The treasure of Samhain was drawing them closer.

Packing the key, they resumed their journey with a newfound sense that something fantastic was in their future. The artifact had not only revealed itself to them but had strengthened their resolve, binding them to a destiny that was unfolding with each step they took. The hidden chamber in the cave was no longer a part of history; it was now a part of them.

The day had grown long, and the shadows stretched out as the trio continued to traverse the puzzling landscape.

Deep in the forest, eyes were watching from the shadows, tracking their every move. Crooked Straw was driven by desire and desperation to be part of the search. As time moved on though, his conviction that he could wear the crown and rule the land weakened. A Vex Shadow, dark and whispery, guided him, promising power and prestige. But within Crooked Straw, the real battle being waged was between two worlds—he felt torn between what he knew was right, and the allure of the dark path.

Sophie, Pierre, and Archibald were making good progress, the ancient artifact secure in a small pouch Archibald wore around his thick neck. But as they ventured into the Whispering Woods, something felt wrong. The air grew tense, the shadows deepened, and an unsettling silence descended.

"I don't like this place," Pierre said, ruffling his feathers. "Something feels off."

"I feel it too," Sophie agreed, her eyes darting. "We've got be cautious."

Archibald's nose twitched and his whiskers bristled. "Stay close," he warned, "and be on your guard."

As they moved deeper into the woods, the twisted branches seemed to reach for them, the whispers growing more pronounced. They moved with caution not realizing what they had walked into. SNAP! It echoed through the air, a net shot out from the undergrowth, ensnaring Pierre.

"Pierre!" Sophie screamed, rushing toward him.

But it was too late. Shadowy figures emerged, grabbing the net and disappeared into the darkness as Pierre's terrified squawks faded into the distance.

"No!" Archibald roared, his eyes ablaze with fury.

Sophie's heart pounded in her chest. "We have to find him!"

The trap had been swift and cunning, the work of someone who knew them well. And as the truth dawned on them, evidence of the scarecrow's involvement lay on the ground near the net, as small pieces of straw declared his presence. Archibald's claws dug into the earth, he sneered, "It's Crooked Straw. He's working with the Vex Shadows."

The realization was a heavy blow, but there was no time to dwell on another betrayal. They had to act, and they had to act fast.

Archibald's badger clan joined them, their faces set with determination. Together, they searched, following the faint trail, guided by the lingering scent of fear and treachery. Hours turned into days as they scoured the dark corners of the Whispering Woods, the urgency growing with each passing moment.

Sophie and the badger clan finally collapsed with fatigue. Sophie put her dirty feathered wings over her face and thought what she would do without Pierre. She'd already lost most of her family. The idea of being alone… it was too much to bear.

Looking up to scan the area, she caught a glimpse of an unusual shape in the distance, a shape that didn't fit in with the landscape of the dense forest. Tired and heartbroken, she almost missed the quirky way he always moved his tail feathers when he was excited or under stress. It was, it was Pierre, tethered to a small tree, his eyes wide with fear. His captors, Crooked Straw among them, were nearby, their voices carrying through the still air.

Sophie's heart ached at the sight of her brother, but she knew they had to be smart. Together with Archibald and his clan, a plan was devised—each move calculated, the stakes higher than ever.

"We'll get him back," Archibald promised, his voice quiet but firm. "We'll make them pay."

Sophie's eyes met Pierre's from a distance, she shook her head, sending him a message only siblings understood, a silent promise of rescue exchanged.

The trap had been laid, the lines drawn, as they prepared to put their plan into action, the weight of the past and the hope for the future hung in the balance. The search for the treasure was no longer a quest; it was a fight for justice, for truth, and for the very soul of the realm. And though Pierre remained captive, his spirit unbroken, the battle had only begun.

Crooked Straw watched from a distance, a dark shadow in the trees. His heart ached with conflict, torn between two worlds.

A Tryst with Treachery

Sophie's eyes narrowed as she peered through the dense underbrush, observing Pierre's captors with a blend of concern and determination.

Archibald crouched next to her in the shadow of the dense forest, their eyes fixed on the clearing where Pierre was tethered. Crooked Straw paced back and forth, his face contorted with internal conflict, the Vex Shadows swirling around him like dark coils of confusion.

Archibald's claws dug into the earth, his snout twitching with suppressed anger.

"Crooked Straw is there," Sophie whispered, her voice quivering with trepidation. "I see him, and those horrible Vex Shadows." Sophie's mind raced, unable to focus. Archibald, seething at his enemies, acknowledged the shadow's presence.

Without a noise, she took flight, staying low to avoid being seen to a branch not far from the clearing. Archibald turned, alarmed that she would leave without committing to an action to recover her brother. As he watched her low-slung flight path, he realized she needed to think, unhindered by the evolving situation in front of them.

Sitting on the branch, her back turned from the clearing and any visual of her brother trapped and held, she thought, *"It's as if the Shadows and Crooked Straw want us to come and get him."* She pondered the circumstance and remembered a lesson Babu had taught them so many years ago. *"Urgency is often coupled with hasty decisions. Stop. Breathe, and allow your inborn instincts to survive rule your choices,"* his rustling leaves then quieted. Not fully understanding his words at the time, now permeated her thinking. *If there was ever a time for using our instincts, this is it.*

A weight lifted from her; the plan began to emerge from deep within her feathered frame.

Flying back to Archibald and his clan, she divulged her thoughts and why she knew this was a trap. "They want us to charge in and release him. That's why he is in this clearing, easy to see, easy for them to capture us." Sophie then laid out her plan, more than only releasing Pierre, a plan for survival. The badger interjected his expertise in retrieval.
This was not the first time he and his clan were caught up in a rescue.

Their strategy in place, they moved to their respective positions and waited, patient as she had learned. The precise time to act would reveal itself by the ill-witted Shadows and the now disgraced Crooked Straw.

"Pierre's strong," Sophie whispered to herself, her voice tinged with urgency and an underlying fear she and the badger would fail. "I can't…. I will not lose my only family to these unseen enemies." Her words sounded hollow in her head. Again, shaking off self-doubt, set her growing confidence to win this battle. The stakes were high for her and Pierre, but the circumstance they found themselves in was beyond mere safety for the two, it was to restore an entire realm back to its glory. She would not fail!

The age-old key, draped around her neck with a piece of twine the badger found in his small pouch, had shown itself to the trio as if another sign they were destined to secure the treasure for the rightful ruler. The beautiful stones that adorned its centerpiece, made of Sardis, Chalcedony and Topaz were set ages ago. Their beauty was mesmerizing as Sophie gazed on them. "These will surely produce the necessary effect," she spoke to herself. Her position, settled beyond a crystal-like pond set opposite to Pierre's captors.

Archibald was closer to the clearing, waiting for the right moment to enact their plot. The sun descended toward the horizon as the two waited in nervous silence. His thoughts went back to his ancestors and the writings engraved upon the coarse walls of that sacred cavern. The two birds hadn't noticed the profound effect those old etchings and inscriptions had on him. Another layer added to this unfolding story of good and evil. He remembered learning the same strategies from his father and his clan, the clan he now led. Hearing his father's voice, *"Watch your enemy, take note of how they act and react before the battle begins. Never respond in haste, but when you do, fight like it will be your last."*

His outward demeanor of knowledge and confidence covered what he felt inside his head and heart. Not feeling worthy or capable in this quest. Archibald was lost in his thoughts, *"this is not about feelings but about what is true, there is no lack in my purpose or my confidence, the Shadows will not use their devious schemes to confuse me and challenge who I am."* Caught up in this moment of introspection, his mind wandered to stories retold around 'the circle of life' his tribe held each full moon.

They retold the myth as told to them by their forefathers, Archibald heard it as if it were told yesterday.

"During the time of Samhain, when the realms of spirit world and physical world converge, the passage between them became easier. Spirits, both kind and malevolent acted with more power in our physical world. Remember the Second Battle of Moytura, a pivotal moment in our past, the battle, fought between the spirit beings, the Vex Shadows, and the Fomoire, including the human and the physical beings who called this land home. The veil between them lifted during that battle, and the Vex have come and gone for centuries. When the veil last closed, three days into the festival of Samhain they remained and have been here ever since sunrise the third day. They are a scourge and must be defeated." The badger's thoughts raced through his mind at lightning speed, solidifying his resolve to rid these unwanted spirits back to the otherworld from where they came. It would only happen on the Night of Samhain and only if we can find the secret treasure. His hopes and the hopes of all the living hinged on their success.

Archibald was brought back to the present as the sun moved in perfect alignment for Sophie to reflect the sacred key at the small army of Shadows and Crooked Straw. The illuminated clearing from the key's reflection off the pond had its intended effect. In the clearing, Crooked Straw's head snapped up, his eyes widening with alarm. The Vex Shadows twisted and turned, drawn to the flash of light, their whispery forms swirling with confusion. Unable to exist in the light, they vanished in a moment. The straw man was exposed and now alone in the shadows near the clearing.

The speed the Shadows disappeared had both Archibald and Crooked Straw astounded. At that very moment, the badger began to burrow his series of underground vibrations, thundering, causing Crooked Straw to lose his sense of orientation. The badger saw his opening and pounced at the traitor.

A Tough Lesson

When Sophie arrived at the edge of the clearing where Pierre was held captive, she observed a scene that brought her to a stark realization—their once simple adventure of parties and treasure had become a nightmare.

The badger had Crooked Straw pinned against a large tree, his eyes threatening to tear the straw man to pieces. With his thick neck and sharp teeth bared at the cringing straw man, it forced a panicked scream from Crooked Straw. "NO. Don't do this!"

The sound of his voice was now different from the first days of their entrance into this strange world. The calm enigmatic old soul was now a shell of his once confident, statuesque self as he reeled at the sight of this angry creature who was ready to attack him.

"Stop!" Pierre's voice reverberated in the once tranquil scene.

Crooked Straw's attention, drawn away from the badger, cast his eyes on Sophie.

"Sophie," Crooked Straw growled, his voice filled with anger and surprise. "Get this thing away from me."

"You are in no position to make demands of anyone," Sophie railed at him, her voice filling with a rage she had never known. The deceit and betrayal Crooked Straw committed against her, and Pierre had surfaced a passion from deep inside.

Taken back by the truth behind her words, he had nothing but a stunned silence. "You lied to us. You deceived us. You betrayed our trust in you." Her words cutting deep into his hay filled heart. Leaning into his space, Crooked Straw couldn't sink back into the tree any further. Archibald continued his stance, not backing down from the straw man.

Sophie noticed an acknowledgment in his old button eyes, almost softening as he got a faraway look not wanting to face the truth. Caught between two worlds, trying to work both to his benefit, he became an easy target for the Vex Shadows to control.

Sophie became convinced that because of his actions and his willingness to be used by the shadows, Crooked Straw was unable to make any sort of rational decision. The Vex had gotten into his head and used his appearance and his status as a mere scarecrow to beat him down, spewing their lies and veiled threats. He believed them. That night he was struck by lightning had deformed more than his body; he had become a pawn to the shadows. They used him as a way to get to Sophie and Pierre and then the map.

Sophie continued, "Where is our map, Crooked Straw? I want it now." She waited intently staring at him. He turned his head away from her gaze and she knew that the Vex Shadows had taken it from him.

She backed away in disgust of the vile straw man she once trusted. By this time, the badger had moved off his stance and retreated to the edge of the clearing, untethering Pierre. Grateful and freed from his restraints, Pierre hugged Sophie with great relief and whispered something in her ear, she turned and gave him an odd but understanding look.

Sophie looked at the badger, her words of gratefulness escaped her, she put her wing on his fury shoulder and looked into his eyes, he nodded in acknowledgement. He understood the silent thank you for his help rescuing Pierre. Sophie and Archibald left for a predetermined spot near an opening in the brush that led to a small stream. As they made their way to the edge of the whispering woods, Sophie's mind replayed the look in Crooked Straw's eyes—the conflict, the longing for something more. Their quest was far from over, and the shadows were growing deeper. But in that moment, she knew that they were on the right path, guided by something stronger than cunning or guile—faith in each other, and a belief in the power of good over evil.

Pierre remained back and spoke to Crooked Straw for several minutes. The straw man listened, shook his head several times in what appeared to be not only understanding, but acceptance. Pierre then turned and flew off. Crooked Straw remained, paralyzed with fear and indecision, knowing the Vex would return as dusk approached. He couldn't hide and he couldn't face them anymore. Wrecked by his own greed, he set his bent body on a rock near the clearing where he had tied Pierre to a branch. He waited and considered Pierre's words. It seemed that all hope was lost to him.

The badger set off in a direction North of their current position, they agreed to meet in two days not far from the secret cave. There was an opening to a large valley behind a hill Archibald had described in detail to Sophie. She committed the place to memory. Pierre caught up with Sophie soon after leaving Crooked Straw.

Their wings beat in unison as they scanned the unfamiliar wilderness, their eyes searching for a clue, a direction. The air was thick with the scent of damp earth and decaying leaves, and their hearts weighed down by the sting of betrayal.

Flying for what seemed like hours, they finally landed on a twisted branch at the base of a rock covered slope that led up to the crest of a small hill. Emotion got the best of Pierre. The stress and excitement of the past week had shaken him. His beak quivered as frustration and a sense of defeat was written all over his face. "I thought I was done, Sophie. I did. I couldn't see a way to get out of the grip of the Vex, and I wasn't confident you and the badger could find me. Thank goodness they tied me where they did. The pond was in perfect position to blind the shadows, and that Crooked Straw is not very clever. But now, I can't see anything. It's like we're blind." Sophie fluttered down beside him; her eyes filled with compassion. "We're not blind, Pierre. We need to see differently."

"What do you mean?" Pierre snapped, his voice rising with irritation.

Sophie looked at him, her voice calm and soothing. "We know our goal is the treasure, hidden away in some abandoned mansion out there." She raised a tired wing with a wave toward the vast forest. "Do you remember the stories Archibald told us? Stories of how the clan defeated their enemies in battle. Battles against larger forces who sought to steal the treasure of Samhain."

Pierre gave her a thoughtful look, recounting that day in the hidden cave. The markings of a civilization that once held reign over the land. He nodded and listened more intently as Sophie continued. "He said those victories happened because they gave all their attention to the predicament in front of them, not what could happen should they fail. We need," she stopped, "we must put our effort toward our next goal, finding the location of our friend and his clan. We've been looking with our eyes this entire journey, thinking about the treasure—but I sense we need to see with our hearts.

We're seeking something greater than the treasure, but we must follow what's right in front of us."

Pierre sighed, his feathers drooping. "But how do we do that? How do we see with our hearts?"

"I don't know exactly how that works, but each time we've needed direction, from somewhere it comes. From Crooked Straw to the badger, even those disgusting Vex Shadows have, unwittingly given us clues," Sophie answered. "For now, little brother, we need to get to that opening in the valley Archibald told us about."

As the sun lost its battle with the night, Sophie and Pierre flew to the top of the slope and found themselves perched on a rocky ledge overlooking a sprawling valley. The mysterious forest lay ahead, but their thoughts were elsewhere. They were silent, weighed down by a feeling they hadn't spoken about in years.

"Sophie," Pierre finally broke the silence, his voice quivering. "Why do you think we keep going on these journeys? It's not only about adventure, is it?" She looked at him, her eyes filled with a longing that mirrored his own. She spoke softly, "No, it's not about adventure."

They both knew the truth, a truth they buried deep within them. A void that haunted them ever since their family disappeared all those years ago. That emptiness had driven them to explore, to seek answers, to fill a void that seemed to grow with each passing day.

"You remember how Mama used to tell us stories?" Sophie's voice was soft, filled with nostalgia. "Stories about brave heroes, magical lands, and hidden treasures. Those stories were more than tales. They were lessons."

"Lessons?" Pierre's eyes widened.

Sophie nodded. "Lessons about courage, about believing in something greater than ourselves, about never giving up hope. Mama always said the answers we seek are out there, waiting for us. These journeys, this quest for the treasure of Samhain, is our way of trying to find those answers."

Pierre's eyes misted. He looked away, the pain of their loss still raw. "Do you think we'll ever find them, Sophie? Our family? The answers to what happened?"

Sophie reached out, touching Pierre's wing. "I don't know, Pierre. But I do know that we have to try. We owe it to them, and to ourselves."

They sat in silence, the weight of their purpose settling around them. The need for adventure was only part of it. Driven by a yearning to understand, to reconnect with a part of themselves they had lost.

The moon began to rise, casting a silvery glow over the valley, and Luna's words echoed in their minds: *"Close your eyes, breathe, and feel the path."*

An easy breeze ruffled their feathers, and a soft glow illuminated the night, Luna, appeared, her eyes sparkling with ageless wisdom.

"You called?" she hooted, landing with the grace that experience brings.

"We didn't call you!" Pierre exclaimed, surprised.

Luna chuckled, "Oh, but you did. Your hearts called, and I heard."

The mystery of this place would never be understood by the two hurting parrots, but right now they didn't need understanding, they needed direction.

Sophie's eyes widened. "Can you help us, Luna? We're lost."

Luna looked at them, her gaze piercing. "Are you lost—or have you only lost sight of why you began this journey?"

Pierre looked down, shame in his eyes. "We want to find the treasure. We want to restore the realm."

Luna's eyes softened. "Those answers will come. But you must trust, not only in others but in yourselves. Close your eyes, breathe, and feel the path."

Sophie and Pierre closed their eyes, their chests rising and falling. Images flashed before them—the mansion, the path, the whispers of the forest guiding them.

Pierre's eyes snapped open. "The forests beyond the whispering woods! That's where we must go!"

Luna smiled. "You see, you knew all along."

Sophie and Pierre looked at each other in awe and amazement at the mystery of this land. When they turned to thank her, she was gone. Not a swirl of feathers, not a noise.

They found themselves needing sleep more than anything. Tomorrow, they would set their course. The path was clear now.

The Ancient Crystal

Sophie and Pierre sat atop the rocky ledge; eyes wide with disbelief at the spectacle before them. The expanse of the valley below bathed in a brilliant sunrise; the golden glow seemed to fill their hearts with an unspoken promise. It was as though they could taste the beauty of the moment. Today was a new dawn in their search for the secret treasure of Samhain. On this clear, clean morning, it was a welcome change from the intensity and heaviness with which they'd been living. They prepared for the next stage of their excursion, taking small portions of apples and seeds.

From a corner of the Whispering Woods, a flash caught their eyes. It was a fleeting spark, a tiny glimmer, yet it grabbed their attention. Their hearts light, the wise Luna's words echoed in their minds: *"Close your eyes and feel the path."* It was a guidance they had come to trust, a mystical compass guiding them through the unknown.

Glancing at each other, and as only brother and sister understood, together they spread their wings and flew into the sprawling valley below. Catching updrafts in the open space, they soared high. The journey was long and filled with uncertainty, but their energy and sense of excitement prompted them forward. The Whispering Woods had always been a place of perplexity, a maze of shadows and secrets, where reality often intertwined with the magical.

They flew on.

As the sun dipped toward the horizon in the late afternoon, they arrived at the location where the reflection was seen, searching for an object that didn't belong. Hidden among the vines and brush, a mirror leaned against a small bush, its edge sparkling with a mysterious light. Sophie and Pierre stood transfixed before the mirror, the vines and brush cleared away to reveal an ancient frame adorned with puzzling engravings. The mirror's dirty surface seemed to shimmer with a life of its own, inviting them to look deeper.

Clearing away more of the remaining debris, they walked around the strange piece and discovered the mirror was not a simple looking glass, but an ancient, multi-faceted crystal. They each looked into a different facet and saw a different reflection. A mesmerizing story played out with each razor-edged angle. It was as though they were watching themselves replaying a different past. Their journey was mapped out in hazy detail, each surface a different viewpoint of their memories.

They squinted in an attempt to focus on the dirty pock marked surface. Their reflection morphing into images that became spellbinding, almost hypnotizing.

They saw themselves overcoming obstacles set by Crooked Straw and the Shadows with a courage they hadn't realized they possessed. The Whispering Woods unfolded its secrets, each twist and turn bursting with new revelations.

Stepping to the back of the strange object they looked around, sensing this may be a trap, but not one animal or strange ethereal being was seen, heard, or smelled. They shot a quick glance at each other to confirm they were not seeing things, that they were not going crazy, and what the mirror possessed was showing a story they had lived out themselves.

There were moments of struggle, of facing the Vex Shadows, and the cunning deception of Crooked Straw. But there were also moments of joy, camaraderie, and the pure elation of discovery. The badger clan, once seen as mythical creatures, were now allies, guides, and friends.

The mirror then revealed them discovering the hidden key, a golden artifact buried within the roots of an ancient oak.

"Do you remember that moment?" Pierre asked, his voice soft and reflective. "I felt something stir within me then."

Sophie replied, her eyes distant as if in a daydream, "What moment?" She was watching an entirely different scene being played out.

She saw herself talking with their parents, barely visible, like they were at the end of a long foggy tunnel. She put her feathered wings on the dirty surface trying to get closer. Not quite able to hear, their words garbled,

they seemed to ask her questions. Sophie turned her head and leaned into the mirror, attempting to make sense of what they were saying. As she lost her focus, they were gone, she was left looking at her own reflection.

Startled, she stepped back, closed her bright blue eyes, and forced herself to recall the memory. But it was lost. She had listened to those muffled voices and couldn't recall what they said, but it must have happened; it was a clear and real memory.

She looked at Pierre and wondered, why the vision of her parents? She paused, and put that pain back, hidden deep inside her heart.

Their reflection continued, each showing a different point of view in their meeting with the badger clan, keepers of the treasure's secrets. The crystalline glass seemed to show the young birds a scene they wanted to remember. They heard their own voices echoing from the mirror, the questions they asked, and the insight they had received. Pierre heard the words of the badger: *"You are on a path of destiny, trust your instincts and the path will be revealed."* Learning to have confidence in his convictions, knowing how much he didn't know or understand was a hurdle directly in front of him. He thought about how courage without understanding could lead to either treasure or capture. Smiling to himself, he chose treasure.

The reflection shifted, both birds now seeing the same memory—the battle with the Vex Shadows, the harrowing clash that had tested the courage and resolve of all who were in the battle. They saw themselves fighting side by side, their faces etched with determination and fear.

"We almost lost ourselves there," Sophie murmured, recalling the dark tendrils that had tried to ensnare them.

A shudder ran down Pierre's spine as he recalled himself caught, taken deep into the woods and tied in a clearing as if he were bait for an even more sinister trap.

The mirror then unveiled the moment of restoration for Crooked Straw, the straw man who had once deceived them but had later sought compassion. "Crooked Straw's voice rang out from the mirror. "I…" he stumbled, lost for words, "deceived. Now I wish to… to find my way back." The vision in the mirror culminated in the discovery of the treasure, a chest overflowing with jewels and ancient artifacts lost for centuries. They saw themselves awestruck and humbled, standing before the riches.

"Was finding this treasure our calling?" Sophie asked, tears in her eyes.

"It's more than the treasure," Pierre answered, his voice filled with confidence. "It's the journey, the lessons, and the friendships. That's the real treasure!"

The scene in the mirror was a grand celebration, a feast held in their honor, attended by all the creatures of the Whispering Woods. They saw themselves dancing, laughing, embraced by a community that had once been hidden from them.

"We did it, Sophie!" Pierre said, a triumphant smile on his face.

"We did," Sophie agreed, her voice filled with contentment.

The treasure of Samhain was not a chest of riches; it was the story of their lives, a tale still in process, a tale they determined to live.

As they watched, the tone of the story shifted, growing more celebratory. The key to the treasure was brought out, the treasure's chamber opened. The Vex Shadows were vanquished to the portal from which they came, and Crooked Straw was given another chance to repair the damage he caused.

They looked at each other, knowing that they were ready to follow the path the mirror had laid out for them. The Whispering Woods were calling. Sophie and Pierre's hearts swelled with emotion as they saw themselves celebrated as heroes. The images in the mirror danced with joy and triumph, they felt a profound connection to something greater, something beyond themselves.

The vision in the crystal faded, back to the dirty old mirror they first found. They stood together, their faces glowing with the realization of what they had seen. The mirror had not shown them the past; it had revealed the essence of their journey, the growth they had undergone, the bonds they had formed.

Sophie and Pierre looked at each other, eyes shining with joy. They knew the mirrored story was not merely a reflection of the past but a guide to their future.

The treasure of Samhain was within their grasp. They set off, knowing they were part of a story still unfolding, a story that would resonate in the Whispering Woods for generations to come.

The sun had set, the stars began to sparkle, mirroring the shine in Sophie and Pierre's eyes. Their path was clear and the adventure far from over. It was just the beginning of a legendary tale that would be told and retold—a tale of courage, friendship, and triumph.

The Red Feather

The rising sun awakened the slumbering birds. From the edge of the Whispering Woods, Sophie and Pierre viewed the immense expanse they had flown over the day before. While they munched on the fruit and seeds that they carried with them, the valley of corn and pumpkin fields illuminated by the Autumn sun reminded them of their first day in this strange land.

Nonstop hours of flight had used all the energy the two had. Still tired, they found their second wind, energized by the thought of the celebration that was to come.

As their visions in the multifaceted mirror faded, leaving Sophie and Pierre standing in stunned silence, the whispering of the ancient trees the only sound in their ears. Anticipating the upcoming journey, they pondered the reflections they had seen. It was like a wild dream, showing both their past triumphs and the future's dazzling promise.

Turning to her brother, she said, "We're going to be heroes, Pierre!" her eyes sparkling with excitement.

"It felt so real, Sophie. But how could it know our future?" Pierre's question gave them a moment to pause and consider the magic the strange land possessed.

"It must be a sign," Sophie replied, her voice full of hope. "A sign that we're on the right path."

While looking for the positive, they basked in the warmth of their imagined success, neither noticed the lurking shadows behind neighboring trees, nor the glint of malicious eyes keeping surveillance over them.

Their path led them, each clue bringing them closer to the abandoned mansion they had seen in the mirror. The scratchy images in the old crystal gave them a direction to go. Though like a mirage, the picture of an actual place etched into their minds.

"With the badger's help," Sophie chirped, "the treasure vault, the defeat of the Vex Shadows and Crooked Straw, it is no longer impossible. Pierre, we can do this."

The forest, once filled with dread and mystery, seemed to beckon them forward, promising adventure and glory. They laughed and joked, their hearts light with anticipation.

The siblings ventured further into the deepest part of the ancient forest, their wings still tingling from the magical mirror's revelations. A tapestry of past triumphs and future victories danced in their minds, filling their hearts with hope.

As they followed a narrow path through the mysterious forest, Pierre's keen eyes spotted something caught in a bush not far off the trail twisting in the soft breeze. A red feather, blushing against the shadows. "What's this?" Pierre asked, his hear quickened picking up the feather with a delicate talon. "It's kind of like ours. I thought for a moment it belonged to..." his voice trailed off.

Sophie's eyes widened as she gazed at the feather, the questions that lay dormant began to stir in her heart. She quickly pushed those issues back down, buried and out of her memory. They kept coming up no matter the effort of her will to stop them. Finally, she asked, "Do you remember, Pierre? The day our parents disappeared?" Her voice trembled with a strange mix of excitement, dread, and fear. "Could this feather be a clue? It must mean we're on the right path."

Pierre's feathers ruffled, his eyes growing distant. "I've thought about that day so many times, Sophie. It haunts me. They were there in the morning, we set off for the baobab tree," he paused. "In my mind it happens so fast, one moment they were there and when we returned, gone." His emotions of guilt and pain and loss began to show. His tears now flowing, "I can't help but feel that if I had been more alert, more watchful, they'd still be with us."

Sophie's eyes flashed, she pounced on Pierre pinning her younger brother to the ground, her wings flapping wildly. "No!" she screeched; her voice filled with an unnerving passion. "You are NOT to blame for our parents being gone! How dare you even think that!" Calming herself, the ache still fresh in her heart, she let Pierre up. "We both have been lost since that day. If it weren't for Babu, our home, we too would have been lost. There is an answer somewhere, little brother, we will find it."

Pierre stared at his sister shocked by the intensity in her eyes. Her words hung in the air, a storm of emotion that rocked them both.

"I'm sorry, Sophie," Pierre stammered, his voice breaking. "I just can't shake the feeling that I failed them somehow."

Sophie's anger melted into sadness, and she pulled Pierre close, tears glistening in her eyes. "We both miss them, Pierre. But we can't lose ourselves in guilt and regret. We've got to use our pain, our longing, to fuel our search for answers."

They sat in silence, the weight of their shared loss bearing down on them, their connection to each other deepening in the shadows of the old forest.

Pierre finally broke the silence, his voice filled with a fresh insight. "You're right, Sophie. It seems our explorations are more than silly adventures. Deep down, we have been on a search for answers, for understanding. This feather, whether it's a clue or not, has reminded us of that."

Sophie nodded, her beak quivering with emotion. "We'll find the secret treasure of Samhain and restore the kingdom to the badger clan, that has to be our focus."

They stood together, the red tail feather now a symbol of their shared mission, a beacon guiding them forward. The magical mirror had shown them a path, but their hearts, bonded by family and loss, were the true motivation leading them onward.

The old woods seemed to whisper back, the trees rustling with secrets and the path stretching out, winding and mysterious. The Vex Shadows and Crooked Straw, the traitor scarecrow, were far away but ever-present, a dark menace lurking just beyond their perception.

With a firm flap of their wings, Sophie and Pierre glided up to a nearby limb getting their bearings. They continued their journey, the memory of the past and the promise of the future urging them forward, their voyage growing in complexity.

They were not treasure hunters; they were seekers of truth, driven by a love that transcended time and space. The old forest had many secrets, but Sophie and Pierre were ready to unravel them, one feather, one step, one heartbeat at a time.

Cloudy With a Chance of Showers

The two birds moved through the intricate forest, they felt a connection with nature, a feeling that emerges over time, yet they felt it now. The magic here was powerful, staying vigilant was a top priority if they hoped to discover the abandoned mansion and its secret treasure. They realized for the first time since they arrived, their longing for Babu and the rainforest. The first twinge of home sickness. The smell of the fires burning, sounds of the monkeys yapping away at nothing.

The magical elements of this strange place had a hold over them, echoing their emotions. "Can you feel it, Pierre?" Sophie asked, her eyes wide with wonder. "The trees, the breeze, everything seems to be speaking to us."

"I can," Pierre responded, his voice tingling with excitement.

The rain began as a sprinkle, a few droplets, landing here and there, soon hitting the ground with loud splats, one pelting Sophie square on her beak.

The smell of rain in the forest is very comforting, the pines and ferns giving off a pleasing clean scent of nature.

As they ventured further into the Whispering Woods, wild gusts of wind began to stir. The leaves whirled and the skies darkened as the wind grew, without warning a storm blew in, the parrots knew they needed to find shelter.

Their enjoyment of the moment was broken as the rain, now blowing sideways with hail the size of acorns began pelting them as the storm raged. Their attempts to fly up under the canopy of the forest got punished by the stout wind, making flying impossible. Their wings, now laden with water, prevented any flight as the rain and wind held them down.

They rushed to get to high ground, the babbling stream they were near became a torrent of raging water. Flash floods happened fast in this land and this one caught them completely off-guard.

The slippery rocks and leaves made reaching any high ground an agonizing trek. Falling, getting up only to fall again, forced the two drenched birds to change course, moving away from the eroding bank of the stream turned river was futile. The elements were too strong and the two slipped into the fast-moving water.

The storm intensified with a ferocity neither Sophie nor Pierre had ever encountered. The clouds seemed to churn with rage as the trees bowed under the weight of the wind. A low rumble, almost like the growl of a beast, echoed through the Whispering Woods. The rain fell, not in droplets but in sheets, blurring the world around them.

Pierre, his heart thumping in his chest, managed to find some grip on a branch that was floating by, clinging to it as the raging floodwaters tried to twist it away from him. The waters swirled and thrashed, making it near impossible to determine up from down.

As the gush of water threatened to engulf him, Pierre felt the branch shift, the current pulling them apart. Sophie's silhouette vanished in the distance, carried away by the watery chaos. His sister's cries lost in the storm. "Sophie!" he called out, his voice raw, but the wind beat down his cry.

With enormous effort, dragging himself toward the water's edge, Pierre managed to scramble to the bank of the now swollen stream. Gasping for breath, his feathers plastered to his body, he scanned the water for any sign of his sister. A tree, one that the storm had uprooted, ensnared the old map in its limbs.

Every instinct screamed at Pierre to retrieve it. It was their lifeline, their guide. He hesitated, torn between the map and searching for Sophie, the surging waters shifted the tree, and the map drifted out of reach.

The map or Sophie? The thought split Pierre's mind, causing a deep anguish. But even as the map teased him, swirling in an eddy as if it were beckoning him, he made his choice. Sophie.

Wings too soaked to take flight, Pierre scampered downstream, the map's enticing call echoing in his ears.

The rain pelted him, each drop feeling like a tiny dagger, blinding him, and slowing his pursuit. He could hardly see a few feet ahead, and with every step, hope seemed to fade. Thoughts raced through his mind: *What if she's hurt? What if I can't find her? What if...?*

He took a moment, resting beside a large moss-covered boulder to shield himself from the worst of the rain, he spotted the map again. It now lay on the opposite bank, ensnared in the roots of a tree, as if it is waiting was its only option. He felt a tug in his heart, a battle of duty against love. The map could change everything for the realm, but Sophie... Sophie was his world.

Pierre took a deep breath, water dripping from his beak, his thoughts swirling as much as the storm around him. "Sophie first," he murmured to himself, determination steeling him. *I'll come back for the map. I have to find Sophie.*

Braving the storm, he continued, hope driving each step, even as his surroundings became unfamiliar. Every wind-blown leaf, every shifting shadow, seemed to whisper of dangers unseen. And all the while, the Whispering Woods watched as ancient as time and equally as unknowable. The journey was risky, but Pierre's determination never wavered, the bond of sibling love pushing him forward.

The roaring deluge carried Sophie further and further away. With every second, the landscape grew less familiar. Towering trees of the Whispering Woods gave way to a more open space. Massive boulders and rocks replaced the once dense foliage, and the glistening stream had become a vicious muddy river, threatening to swallow her whole.

Sophie's talons clutched at a tiny branch that bobbed alongside her, her beak snapping at anything solid in the torrent. With heart pounding in her chest, she allowed the branch to guide her, riding the flow until it pushed her to the waterlogged bank.

Digging her beak deep into the mud, she anchored herself to the root of a withered bush, the wind and water doing their best to pry her away.

As the storm dwindled to a drizzle, the wrath of the flood relented. Sophie, now marooned in a vast and unfamiliar landscape, was a miserable sight. Mud plastered her once radiant feathers, and broken twigs and soggy leaves tangled amidst them.

She sought shelter near a large boulder, trying to make sense of the whirlwind of events that had separated her from Pierre. The burden of loneliness pressed on her heart, each passing second amplifying the dread that she was lost.

To hold off a creeping panic, Sophie attempted to clean her wings, though every touch brought grimaces of pain. The cold, the exhaustion, and the sheer intensity of the ordeal began to take their toll, and her eyes grew heavy. Slumping against the boulder's cold surface, she was soon in the grips of a deep, fitful sleep.

Her dreams were as turbulent as the storm that had brought her to this desolate place. The familiar gloom of the Vex Shadows spread like a plague, consuming everything in its path. Pierre, ensnared in a cage made of darkness, screamed her name, his voice filled with despair.

The abandoned mansion, once a beacon of hope in their quest, was now overrun. Shadows slithered over walls and through corridors, extinguishing every source of light. At the heart of it all, atop a pile of glistening treasure, sat Crooked Straw. His straw-like fingers clutched gleaming jewels, a sinister grin stretching across his face.

It was clear to Sophie, even in the dream, that Crooked Straw was not the true mastermind. Hovering beside him, its form ever shifting, was Shade, the leader of the Vex Shadows. Crooked Straw jabbered on about his greatness and might, but every word seemed hollow, an echo of Shade's whispered desires.

The nightmare reached its pinnacle with Sophie chained and bound, the weight of all their failures insistent in their intent. As the Shadows drew closer, a cold, paralyzing fear gripped her heart.

She jolted awake with a sharp intake of breath. Gazing at the surroundings, reality was almost as disheartening as the dream. The deafening silence of the unfamiliar terrain disrupted by the distant echo of water receding. The once fierce storm had given way to a gray, ugly sky, squashing Sophie's spirits.

Her chest heaved, the nightmare's terror still gripping her. Memories of her and Pierre's close encounters with the Vex Shadows came flooding back, each more harrowing than the last. Sophie again, had doubts about the true reason for coming here. Thinking to herself, imagining she was in a conversation with her mother it struck her. *It's me. I'm to blame.* Her beak quivering, Sophie realized for the first time her accountability. For enticing Pierre to go on these journeys and the ease at which she could pursue getting the answers they wanted, putting her life at risk as well as Pierre's. She wanted answers, so she was willing to risk their safety to find them. Her tears began to roll freely off her light feathered cheeks. Humbled by this realization, she remembered Babu's words, *"… treasure is often hidden for a reason."*

Strengthened by this realization, and knowing what the treasure held, she was emboldened to find the mansion and unearth the passageway to the secret chamber. She hoped Archibald was nearby to ensure the treasure was unlocked by the rightful heir. The night wore on, her thoughts becoming muddled and confusing, her instincts kicked in, I've got to find shelter, I will look for Pierre soon. "I'm out here brother," she whispered to herself.

Lost

The sky was dark and cold and the stars shining through molted clouds and the waxing moon casting shadows over the landscape. The raging waters had littered boulders and piles of broken tree limbs across the ground.

Waking up with a start, Sophie found herself nestled under a muddy brown bush. Not sure how long she had slept, the mud had dried and caked on all over her feathers. She felt weighted down by the extra earth she wore. Using her beak and talons, most of the large chunks came off. By rubbing up against a large rock, she was able to remove the biggest share. Flapping her wings to air them out, pain shrieked through her sides.

Bouncing along a rain swollen stream was an adventure she would check off her to-do list. Cold and hungry, Sophie longed to hear Pierre's voice. Hearing nothing but the distant night noises of the unusual landscape, she waited for dawn to begin her search.

For now, the quiet darkness gave way to strange voices and the continuous replay of that disturbing dream. It dominated her thinking. Unsettling and starting to scare her, Sophie began to let fear creep into her soul. She feared it would come to dictate her fate.

The hours passed; the remnants of her dream began to fade as sleep once again overtook her. There was a spark of cautious determination kindled within her. Would it be strong enough to help the two continue their search? As dawn broke over the landscape, she looked for any sign of a path back to the Whispering Woods, to Pierre, and to their shared mission. It didn't look promising.

Pierre's heart raced as the torrential waters that almost claimed him raged on. Clambering up the riverbank, drenched and shivering, he surveyed the aftermath of the flood. But his thoughts, interrupted by the sight of their map, caught in a mess of twigs and leaves on the other side of the turbulent waters.

Summoning his strength, he shook off the chilling rain and took to the sky, his keen eyes darting to and fro in search of Sophie. The land below bore the scars of nature's fury – trees uprooted, boulders displaced, and an eerie silence replacing the once familiar chirping of birds and rustling of leaves.

Spotting a sunlit clearing in the distance, Pierre decided to secure their map first. He swooped down and with a swift motion, plucked it from its watery prison. He spread the now wrinkled and soaked parchment on a concealed bush, allowing the sun to dry it, its once clear markings now faded.

He once again took to the skies, calling out, "Sophie! Sophie, where are you?!"

His mind was a torrent of its own. *What if she's trapped under the debris? What if she's injured? Or worse...* he shoved the dreadful thoughts away. "She's strong," he muttered to himself. "She must be."

The hours stretched on, the vastness of the Whispering Woods seemed to taunt him, hiding its secrets beneath a canopy of wet leaves and muddied waters. The doom he felt inside intensified, making his wings heavy.

"She could be anywhere," Pierre lamented, voice echoing through the trees, "Lost... or even..." He couldn't complete the thought, the mere idea threatening to crush his spirit.

After an endless search, he found himself back in the clearing, the map now dry but Sophie nowhere in sight. He slumped beside it, exhaustion and despair overtaking him.

"I should've been there for her," he whispered, a tear escaping his eye. "Sophie, if you're out there, please be safe," he said out into the wind.

Hunger gnawed at him, but the void left by Sophie's absence overshadowed any physical discomfort. He imagined her, alone and scared, fighting to find him.

Gathering himself he glanced at their map, the location of the hidden chamber nearly washed away by the muddy water, a thought flashed. "The chamber...

the flood ruined most of this map." The hope it had once symbolized seemed a distant memory, he knew he couldn't give up. "I will find you, Sophie. No matter what it takes," he murmured.

Under a canopy of stars, Pierre lay restless with the cool night air breezing past him. Every rustle, every distant cry in the woods seemed amplified, tugging at his fears. The moonlight threw abnormal silhouettes, and shadows danced around him, playing out his worst imaginings. Every time he closed his eyes, they filled with dark images of Sophie, trapped or injured, calling out to him. Fear overtook him. It wasn't from the Whispering Woods or even the cold ground he nested on, but from the guilt and worry swirling within.

The unforgiving night seemed endless, then finally, as the light of dawn washed over the woods, he prepared for another day of searching, driven by a brother's unyielding love. Pierre was on the move as the sun peeked over the horizon. His sleep-deprived eyes, burning, scanned every inch of the terrain, leaving no stone unturned.

The morning light trickled through the dense canopy, creating a maze of glimmers and glooms. The woods, once familiar, now felt like a perplexing puzzle, twisting and turning at every bend. With each flap of his wings, hope wavered between hopelessness and desperation.

Hours rolled on, the sun climbing higher, casting long, dramatic shadows. Pierre's heart raced with every shadow that resembled Sophie. But every fleeting hope led only to a deflated realization, she was nowhere to be found.

He ventured into a different area of the woods soaring high above the treetops; something caught his eye. Near a muddy bush, there were unmistakable marks—talon prints. A baffling array of emotions surged through him.

Nose diving to the spot, he saw the size and pattern matched Sophie's, and upon closer inspection, he unearthed a single, silvery-gray feather stuck to a broken tree limb with mud. It glistened as if touched by morning dew. It was Sophie's.

His heart skipped a beat. Was this Sophie's way of telling him she was out there alive? With the discovery, the curtain of despair lifted ever so slightly, replaced by a cautious spark of hope. But questions burst forth like a cascade. *Where did she go from here? Why only one feather? Was this a sign of assurance or a distress call?*

The woods, with its mysterious character, whispered back with many voices, none providing any clarity. Still, with the feather held close, Pierre felt reinvigorated.

"I'm coming, Sophie!" he called out, hoping that wherever she was, she'd hear him. The feather, soft against his talons, seemed to pulse with a life of its own—a beacon in the puzzling expanse of the Whispering Woods.

Pushed on by the mix of love, fear, and hope, Pierre surged forward, the dance of shadows and light guiding his way. The Whispering Woods once a source of foreboding now rumbling with the promise of a reunion. With the rhythm of his heart echoing in his ears, Pierre pressed on, led by a feather and an undying hope.

The Abandoned Mansion

The morning of the third day, Pierre's resolve to find Sophie had grown stronger, even as the worry of doubt dragged him down. The sun gave off a hazy glow over the Whispering Woods, making the dense thicket appear even more secretive. Dark clouds rumbled in the distance, another storm brewing. Time was running out.

Both despair and reason bounced inside his head urging him to find a vantage point. Soon, he found himself settling on the tallest tree in the woods. From this height he hoped to glimpse some sign of Sophie or a clue that would lead him to her. As he scanned the vast expanse, his gaze caught something unexpected: set at the edge of a clearing, the grandeur of its past still evident in its hollow structure sat an ancient, abandoned mansion.

His eyes wide in disbelief Pierre whispered, "th….th-the mansion."

There it stood, standing tall and still like an old sentry guarding secrets within its stone walls. Rumors of its treasures and hidden chambers had echoed in hushed tones among the residents of the Whispering Woods. *Could Sophie have headed there?* The thought struck him like lightning, and without delay, he flew towards the old estate, taking care to stay low and hidden from any prying eyes.

The closer he got, the more intimidating it seemed. The tales of its history and mysteries appeared large in his mind. Pierre was cautious, treading the fine line between curiosity and safety. He chose a dense cluster of bushes near the vine covered structure, noting the weird silence that covered the area.

A relic of another era, its imposing gray and brown stone silhouette stood out against the dense green of the woods. Sitting atop a grassy hill surrounded by a moss-covered rampart, he could see the remains of a moat now filled with brush and a collapsed drawbridge, its large stones lay where they fell.

A thick, gnarled vine, had woven its way in and out of the stone walls reaching the tall corner towers, embracing the mansion, providing it with a twisted coat supported by its sturdy walls. Many of the mansion's grand doors were long gone, leaving gaping openings that led into darkness. These empty doorways were like portals to the past.

The smell of damp leaves and old earth gave it a dank and musky scent. It not only looked old, but it also smelled old.

The remnant of a long-gone storm was a massive tree, leaning against a wing of the mansion. The tree once a proud sentinel beaten by nature's fury. Despite the sense of despair, there was an overpowering beauty in the decay, painting it with shades of moss and lichen. The mansion stood as a testament to time.

Has anyone seen me? Could Sophie be inside? Or is it a trap? The thoughts ricocheted inside Pierre's head, creating a storm of indecision. He felt the need to act, to do something, but the fear of the unknown paralyzed him.

A slight murmur caught his attention. Moving silently, he found a concealed perch on the back wall of the old structure. There, in a hidden courtyard, stood the last two figures he expected to see together—Archibald the badger, and Crooked Straw the two-faced scarecrow, their heads together deep in conversation.

The scene before him felt like a twisted nightmare. Words floated up to him, snippets of a conversation that hinted at betrayal, power, and the treasure of Samhain. He could see that Archibald still had the key to the treasure around his thick furry neck.

Pierre felt the old wall beneath him shift. The foundations of trust and loyalty on which he had built his beliefs seemed to crumble. He felt a rush of emotions: anger, disbelief, sadness, and an overwhelming sense of betrayal.

What does this mean? Why is Archibald with him? Have they both deceived us? Where does this leave Sophie and me? The questions tore through him, each more agonizing than the next.

It wasn't only the immediate danger that pierced him, but the realization that the stories of heroism and bravery, the tales that had inspired their quest, were now intertwined with lies and deceit. In this moment, the mansion wasn't a structure of stones and secrets; it was a mirror that reflected the deceit of those Pierre thought he knew.

His mind struggled with the revelations he'd witnessed. Confusion and a pain gripped him. He had to find Sophie, but now he needed to move with care, knowing friends could be enemies. He whispered to himself, seeking comfort in his own voice. "We've faced shadows and storms before. We can face this treachery, too."

The mansion stood as a witness to countless battles and tales from centuries past, Pierre couldn't get rid of the feeling that this ancient, vine covered mass was about to become part of his own story.

Drawing a deep breath, he decided he couldn't confront them now, not without Sophie by his side. The treasure of Samhain, while vital, was secondary. He needed to find his sister and together, they would decide their next move.

With a heavy heart but a clear mind, Pierre retreated to a safe ledge in the tallest tower of the mansion, his mission now two-fold: to reunite with Sophie and unearth the depth of the betrayal.

The Reunion

Dappled sunlight filtering through its dense foliage, the Whispering Woods stretched far into the horizon. At its heart lay an abandoned mansion once regal yet now standing silent in its decaying glory. The dilapidated structure held Pierre perched high on a stone ledge, his sharp eyes watching the shadowed alcove below. There, in the center of crumbling walls, Archibald the badger whispered secrets to Crooked Straw. Pierre's heart raced, pulsing against his feathery chest as he tried to grasp the weight of the scene unfolding below.

"Archibald?" Pierre whispered, the hurt and growing confusion evident in his voice. "Why?" The previous encounters with the badger, always rooted in trust, now screamed of deceit. This covert meeting shifted the ground beneath Pierre's talons. The questions raged in Pierre's mind, *what were the true motives of the badger? If Crooked Straw was here, then were the Vex Shadows far behind?* His head spun, swirling around with these thoughts he felt confused and paralyzed, unable to make any sort of decision or even move. Shaking his head, he snapped out of his stupor and realized he needed to find Sophie before any plan could be enacted.

*****

As the sun began to rise on the third day of her solitary journey, Sophie—strangely drawn to the melodic chorus of forest birds—forged on, their song guiding her. She became increasingly aware of every rustling leaf, every shadow, and every distant echo that resonated within the Whispering Woods. Ancient, magical, and full of hidden tales and secrets the trees whispered to each other when the winds blew.

Sophie, stained with mud on her feathers, encountered a small clearing where an old, chattering squirrel sat on top of a moss-covered stump. Curious, she approached the squirrel, and in her gentle voice she inquired, "Excuse me, Mr. Squirrel, have you happened to see a creature, like me, passing by?" Twitching his bushy tail the squirrel spoke in a squeaky whistly kind of voice, "Ash of metter o'fact, I seen one a'liken to you a day back. He was headed off in the direction ooof an old trail used by some ooof us animals durin' our nightly prowls." He cleared his little voice and told her what she needed to hear. "It leads to an old mysterious mansion. Probly no more 'en a half days flight fer you." Elated, Sophie thanked the squirrel and took flight toward the trail.

Using the trail as her guide, she ventured deeper into the woods until the canopy became too thick for her to see. She walked the path, keeping a wary eye out for the shadows, Crooked Straw, and the badger. Soon, the path began to change, from well-worn earth and leaves to ancient cobblestones that peeked through the overgrowth. This route, once well-trodden, lined with majestic trees as old as time itself. Their gnarled roots creating mossy steps and greenish brown archways that Sophie marveled at.

As she ventured deeper into the woods, the more evidence of a previous culture showed itself. Crumbled stone statues of mythical creatures and family crests lay beneath thick ivy and moss. The scent of mystery and damp earth filled her head with tales of grandeur and decayed decline. *What is this place?* she thought. What she envisioned in her head bore no resemblance to what she was seeing and feeling now.

After hours of trekking, the thick canopy of trees finally gave way to reveal a grand silhouette of the abandoned mansion. Sophie's heart swelled with a mixture of anticipation and anxiety. She was certain that if Pierre were anywhere in the Whispering Woods, he would be drawn to this place as she had been. Clutching a lone red feather, she'd found earlier—a sign of Pierre's presence—she approached the mansion, staying well back from any vantage point someone or something hidden, watching. She spied a nook near the top of the ancient structure, hidden from view but still offering a look from above.

As she arrived, she saw him—Pierre peering down into the courtyard of the mansion. She had no sooner landed when he took flight to the top of the tallest tower. There he sat, a confused look on his face. She needed to get to him, but fearful of who or what may be in the courtyard would see her, she waited.

As twilight began to fall, Sophie gathered her courage and was trying to decide if it were safe to fly to the tower where her brother sat, perched behind a large broken brick. With a quiet flap of her wings, she flew up to where her brother sat. Pierre, still consumed by the shock of the meeting, sensed a presence nearby. Turning, his eyes me Sophie's. Words failed them both as they clung to each other, feathers mingling, relief washing over them. The weight of the past days, the fear of loss, and the trauma of separation was all forgotten in the elation of their reunion.

After some time, they each filled in the past three days, culminating with Pierre's story of Archibald and Crooked Straw. Realizing their position was not the safest, they retreated to a nearby tree to rest, plan, and execute what was to become legend in this strange land they had fallen into.

The Plan

With Archibald and Crooked Straw no longer in view from their perch, the two parrots ventured toward the mansion's entrance. Its grandeur, though faded, was evident. Mighty pillars, moss and lichen-covered statues, and ancient tapestries, now in decay, painted a vivid picture of the mansion's illustrious past.

The mansion, similar to a time when the realm thrived in a sensation of magic and folklore, appeared ahead. Nestled in the very heart of the land, it carried the legacy of its Celtic origins proudly, almost defiantly, against the passage of time. Every stone, every crevice, seemed to hum with tales of old; tales whispered among the trees of the Whispering Woods, carried forward by the winds of time.

As the birds approached the entrance to the ancient, castle-like structure, they were met with a grand façade that seemed to stretch endlessly into the sky. Towering above were battlements and turrets, built with attention to detail. Rusted gates, now fallen but once stately, held intricate designs of mythical creatures tangled in endless Celtic knots.

Beyond the gates, a courtyard sprawled, giving the first hints of the mansion's expansive scale. But it was the main entrance that caught Sophie and Pierre's attention immediately. Two massive pillars, worn by weather and age, stood guard. These were not just simple stone structures; they carried the weight of history. Engravings depicting legendary battles, moments of peace, and scenes from everyday life portrayed on their lengths.

Nearby the entrance were statues, grand and imposing, but now softened with a carpet of moss and lichen. They seemed to come alive under the muted sunlight, their stony gazes appearing both mournful and regal. Each statue narrated a story—a king with his crown, a maiden with her harp, warriors with their weapons, all frozen in time but echoing an era where valor and honor were the realm's currency.

Sophie and Pierre's wide eyes took in all the entrance had. Their imaginations ripe with the stories the statues told.

But it was the interiors that took their breath away. The vast hallway was lined with ancient worn tapestries, now fraying at the edges, color faded with age. They showcased tales of heroes and heroines, dragons and faeries, all interwoven with the distinctive swirling patterns. These tapestries, despite their decay, seemed to pulse with life, with every thread whispering secrets of an age long gone.

Stained glass windows, mostly broken, filtered in a kaleidoscope of colors, casting dancing shadows that played on the mosaic floors. Every corner of the mansion seemed to echo with memories, making the silence even more overpowering. They came to their senses and remembered they were not on a tour but a mission. They moved quietly to the edges of the grand hallway to conceal their presence. Within this vast display of grandeur and decay, the parrots felt both unimportant and yet deeply connected. They were now part of this tapestry, threading their own story into the mansion's rich history. They knew they had a mission to fulfill, a treasure to find, and a realm's legacy to uphold.

Guided by the map, they navigated through a series of twisted corridors and grand halls. Sophie and Pierre whispered back and forth, puzzling over the map's cryptic clues and symbols.

Pierre traced a claw over the faint, intricate lines, his eyes darting back and forth, attempting to get a sense of the map's layout to the mansion's structure. "See this spiral?" he began, pointing toward a symbol that seemed to be nestled in the heart of the map. "I believe this the grand staircase in the central hall. And if that's the case..." His voice trailed off as he connected several passageways leading from it.

Sophie leaned closer; her gaze fixed on a scribbled mark, located in what appeared to be the mansion's northwest corner. "The chamber must be here," she whispered, excitement evident in her voice. "But see this elaborate path? The chamber's entrance is no doubt concealed and protected somewhere in there."

Pierre nodded in agreement. "This mansion was designed as a fortress of sorts. Whoever built it wanted to ensure its treasures remained hidden. We need a strategy."

Sophie noticed an alternate path, one less direct but empty of potential traps and pitfalls the main route promised. "What if we use the servants' corridors? They would have been designed for discreet movement, hidden from the main halls."

A smile crossed Pierre's beak. "Brilliant, Sophie. The servants would've needed a way to move about unseen, avoiding the main corridors. It's less likely Archibald and Crooked Straw would think of that."

"But" Sophie hesitated, "the servants' corridors might be so decayed getting in there might be impossible. We'd have to be careful."

The two parrots began plotting their course. Pierre remembered a partially obscured door he'd seen earlier, draped in heavy cobwebs. "That could be the entrance to the servants' route," he mumbled almost to himself.

"Once we reach the central hall," Pierre continued, pointing to the spiral on the map, "we'll need to find this hidden doorway. It's probably hidden by all of the fallen sculptures and tapestries, but it should lead us to the northwest section."

Sophie's eyes gleamed with determination. "We need to reach that chamber before Archibald and Crooked Straw."

Pierre tucked the map safely beneath his wing. "It's either luck or fate that we found this place. Crooked Straw was the last to have that part of the map, or even Archibald. They've found the location, what they don't have are directions to the secret chamber."

Thinking to himself, *this old castle is like a maze, without a map or someone to lead you...* Pierre's thoughts fell off. Realizing how exposed they were, he whispered to Sophie, "I think we're being followed, let's scatter a few dropped feathers, an overturned vase—anything that might lead them away from our path and maybe buy us some time."

Sophie nodded and quietly peeped, "A diversion. Perfect."

With their plan in place, the sibling parrots knew teamwork and their wits would be their greatest assets. Ready to delve into the heart of the mansion and uncover long-buried truths, the two weary birds pressed on.

The Chamber

T he passages of the mansion seemed to stretch infinitely, like veins running through the heart of a forgotten world. They clutched their weather-worn map, every ink-stained line a path they must decipher before the arrival of Samhain's first evening. A sacred night when destinies could be rewritten, and the rulers of realms were anointed.

Archibald the badger and Crooked Straw were not far behind, their hurried steps echoing through the endless hallways like drumbeats of an approaching army. Time was running out, and both parties knew it. The moment of reckoning was near, and the mansion itself seemed to sense the urgency, its ancient walls trembling as if anticipating a seismic shift. With each twist and turn, the Triquetra, used to symbolize triune deity on their map became clearer in relation to the mansion's geography. Sophie caught a peculiar marking on one of the doors—a near-forgotten symbol etched into the wood. "This is it, Pierre. The symbol matches!" she exclaimed.

As Pierre nodded, a profound sense of purpose washed over them, as if every moment of their lives had been leading to this.

"Yes, the symbol does match, Sophie." Archibald softly added with a determined look on his face. Both he and Crooked Straw had made the right choice at a series of hallways and found Sophie and Pierre ready to enter the chamber.

Pierre turned angrily, feathers bristled, his beak tightening as he confronted Archibald and Crooked Straw. "I saw you two, deep in conversation, in the courtyard. What game are you playing, Archibald?"

Archibald looked up, his eyes meeting Pierre's with a blend of sorrow and revelation.

"Pierre, it's not what it seems. I was trying to convince Crooked Straw to right his wrongs. He's been misled."

"Misled? He's a traitor, Archibald! He led the Vex Shadows to me. They stole the map," Pierre shot back, his voice trembling with a mixture of anger and betrayal.

"It's true," Crooked Straw interjected, his voice full of remorse. "I've been a puppet in the hands of the Vex Shadows. They promised to release my soul from this scarecrow form, but they tricked me, used me to trap you, Pierre."

Sophie's eyes narrowed. "So, you sacrificed our lives, our quest, for your freedom?"

Crooked Straw hung his straw head low. "I'm so sorry. I was desperate. But the Vex Shadows are merciless. They'll destroy this realm, and I've led them right to its core."

Archibald stepped forward; his voice filled with a newfound authority. "That's why we must get to the chamber before they do. We have the key, and now, the map back in our possession. We have a chance to save the realm from the darkness and oppression it has lived under for too long."

Pierre glanced at Sophie, then back at Archibald and Crooked Straw. "Fine. But Crooked Straw stays with us. If this is a trap, it will be on his conscience forever."

Crooked Straw nodded solemnly. "I can live with that. Well, as much as a scarecrow can live."

Sophie finally broke her silence. "If we're doing this, we're doing it now. The dusk of Samhain is upon us. We don't have any time to waste."

Archibald nodded. "Time is of the essence. The Vex Shadows are close, but they are unaware of the chamber's location. Let's secure the treasure and protect the realm. Are we all in agreement?"

Each nod that followed was an unspoken vow, binding them to the fate of a realm teetering on the edge of light and darkness. This uneasy alliance had become their last stand, and the weight of it hung heavy as they turned to open the door to the depths of the mansion, the chamber that held the realm's last hope on the opposite side of the ancient door.

The treasure chest that lay at the heart of the chamber was no ordinary receptacle. Crafted from ancient oak that had been traced from the mythical Celtic Tree of Life, its wood was etched with intricate patterns of knots and swirls. These symbols were not merely ornamental; they were a cryptic language—signatures of elemental spells and alchemic codes infused into the wood at the time of its crafting. The chest itself was a living testament to the essence of the realm it resided in mysterious, ancient, and filled with a power that surpassed time and matter.

The centerpiece of the chest was a mysterious lock made of intertwining serpents, their emerald eyes glowing softly, the key found by the trio so long ago. Legend had it that the serpents would awaken at the touch of the destined one. What lay within it was said to have the power to bring either prosperity or ruin, depending on who unlocked it. The contents were not simply material treasures, but a combination of the realm's essence: the wisdom of its leaders, the bravery of its heroes, and the dreams of its people, all filled in mystical jewels and artifacts.

Archibald, now draped in the glow of his newfound authority, produced a key that seemed as ancient as the chest itself. The key was not made of any earthly metal but appeared to be carved from an ethereal material that flickered like a celestial flame. Though it had sat heavy around his neck throughout his quest—its gravity a constant reminder of his lineage and the responsibilities that came with it—it now felt almost weightless. As if recognizing its master, the key seemed to hum softly, resonating with the vibration of Archibald's soul.

"It's not just any key," Archibald said, holding it up to the light streaming down from the chamber's otherworldly glow. "It's made from stardust, infused with the essence of this realm. It can only be wielded by one whose intentions are pure, whose honor is untainted, and whose destiny has been ordained by the realm itself. Many have tried to force the lock, all have failed."

Pierre and Sophie looked at each other. Despite the trials they'd faced and the doubts they'd harbored, they could see now that Archibald had been the rightful guardian of this kingdom's legacy all along. The gravity of the moment was profound. If Archibald were indeed the destined ruler, the serpents would yield if not, the treasure would remain locked away, perhaps forever.

As Archibald inserted the key into the lock, the serpents on it seemed to stir, their emerald eyes blinking as if waking from a deep slumber. There was a tense pause, a moment where the air in the chamber seemed to hold its breath. Then, as if recognizing an old friend, the serpents uncoiled, their bodies aligning into a straight path for the key to turn.

The lid of the chest creaked open to reveal an array of artifacts—gemstones that captured the essence of the realm's five elements, a sword forged from the scales of a dragon, scrolls containing the wisdom of ages, and a wealth of seeds representing the realm's untapped potential. All were images for the rich legacy and future promise of this strange and mysterious land the parrots found themselves in.

Archibald closed the lid, locking away the treasure until needed to restore the kingdom once more, everyone present understood that they were witnessing not just the continuation of an old tale but the genesis of a new epoch. It was not just Archibald's lineage but his courage, wisdom, and inherent nobility that had opened the chest. He was indeed the rightful ruler, bound not just by birth but by a sense of honor that was the true treasure safeguarding the realm's future.

Hollow Hills and the Sidh

In a dimly lit cavern at the edge of the Whispering Woods, the Vex Shadows huddled in a slithering nest. Mysterious and menacing, they were dark figments woven from the threads of primeval curses. The revolting mass of evil squirmed in delight as their master, Shade approached. An entity so dark he sucked away any light around him. Beady red eyes glinted lies and deceit as he spoke. His voice coarse and vile, unable to speak without a hiss, an echo sounded, "Archibald hasssh the keeey, and from wwhattt we have heard, only shhomeone virtuous," he paused and let out a wicked laugh that frighted his own clan, "yessh, shhomeone worthy who can use it." His voice began to rise, "Heeesh been a thorn to usssh, but my plan involvesss another duo, those interfering birds, Shhophie and her pesky brother Pierre."

A dark figure named Desolation sneered, "These parrots who've disrupted our schemes? I've been dying to teach them a lesson."

Shade grinned, revealing teeth that glowed against his shadowy form. "Exshactly. We will capsshhure those birds and offer Archibald as trade, the key for their lives. Hissh honor won't prevent him from succumbing to such emosshonal blackmail."

Another shadow, Wisp, nodded. "Yes, my lord. He would forfeit the key to save lives. His integrity is his weakness." The nest of shadows cheered with their eerie snorts of laughter.

Unknown to the Vex Shadows, a counterplot was unfolding. Archibald, Sophie and Pierre, and the now contrite Crooked Straw, had joined together with the strange beings, *aos si*, the magical dwellers of the hollow hills.

In the heart of the whispering woods, hidden within the complex jumble of ancient oaks and shadows, lay the Celtic Hollow Hills. These were not common hills; they were burial mounds, known as Sídh, mystical portals to the "Otherworld." As dusk began to settle over the land, the hills seemed to pulsate with a quiet, unearthly energy as the festival of Samhain drew near.

This ancient race, beings of both light and nature, had watched the advance of darkness on their realm for centuries. Pomona, the goddess revered during Samhain, was their last resort. With her powers reaching their peak during this sacred time, she would banish the Vex Shadows through the Sídh, ghostly portals leading to the "Otherworld." But first, they somehow needed to draw the Shadows to the Hollow Hills.

The fabric between the living world and purgatory was thin, almost transparent. Each mound appeared as a gentle rise, covered with moss and bordered by circles of stones—stones etched with puzzling hieroglyphs and swirls, as if written in a script that danced between a mythical kingdom and the ordinary. Each Sídh was crowned with an ancient marker worn smooth by centuries of rain and wind, its face adorned with Celtic carvings that shimmered in the light that seemed to radiate from the ground during this transitional season.

But it was on Samhain, the night when the veil between worlds lifted, that the Hollow Hills revealed their true splendor. Bonfires could be seen within the

Sídh, flickering flames of a world not our own, casting shadows and light in an eternal dance of celestial interaction. The air, filled with a haunting melody, a ghostly symphony played, reaching into the deepest recesses of the soul. On this sacred night, the Aos sí—people of the hills—would emerge to oversee the solemn rites and rituals that would secure the realm's future. Here, in this mystical setting, miracles and treacheries made next to one another, would fulfil the destiny of this land.

Standing in these hills was like the crossroads of past, present, and future. Those brave enough to go near them could get a glimpse through a doorway to a different dimension, seeing but not understanding mysteries unsolved and destinies unwritten.

As dusk settled the first night of Samhain, the Sídh were unsealed; an unearthly sensation surrounded the stage. The setting was mystical, dreamlike, Sophie looked at Pierre for a moment, her expression unyielding, eyes fierce with conviction. "We have come too far to be pawns in the Shadow's deceit." Her voice woven together with an assurance she wished she felt. "We know the desperation the Shadows must take possession of the key. If this succeeds," she paused, realizing what both her and Pierre were about to commit to, "when this succeeds, the realm will be free from centuries of tyranny, the fight is worth the risk." Her words sounded more confident than she felt. She remembered the words of Luna: *"Feelings are momentary; it's truth that endures."* Sometimes, the truth was hard to follow.

It was dusk as the group dispersed to set their trap. The parrots fluttered toward a clearing, an open space near the hollow hills, visible to any spies the Shadows might have lurking. As expected, they were seized by shadowy creatures and brought before the Vex Shadows.

In the moments before twilight, Sophie and Pierre found themselves face-to-face in a confrontation with Shade, the devious leader of the Vex Shadows. The mist hung low, and the ghostly fires from the Sídh flickered like distant stars, casting a strange glow on the scene. Shade's formless face loomed closer, attempting to envelop the young parrots in a cloud of fear.

"Ah, the famousssh avian sshiblingsz," Shade cooed, his voice dripping with an oily sweetness that turned the stomach. "You'fff been interfering it mattersssh that don't conshhern you, isshn't that correct?" Not waiting for an answer, the vile spirit continued, "but I'm a generoussh leader. Give me the keeey, and I promissshe, you'll both go free." The entity, consumed with himself and the evil that possessed him, oozed a retched smell of dank sulfur. His power over the land was based on lies and the confusion he and his followers could twist into half-truths. His skill at this deceit was the reason he led the Vex Shadows and controlled the realm for so long. He continued, "a new age issh coming to thissh realm, one way or another." The darkness moved in, his face a swirling abyss, close to the young birds, "you wouldn't want to be on the wrong sshide of hisshtory."

The two young parrots willed themselves to not show the fear that they felt growing inside. Glancing at each other, a momentary thought crept into Sophie's mind: *What have I gotten us into?* But it was gone and forgotten as quickly as it arrived. She had a flashback of her trip down the river, dodging rocks and tree limbs and the conversation she had with herself about guilt. A voice came to her, not anything she could hear, but a voice inside her heart, "You are stronger than you know."

Sophie would need that declaration of truth sooner than later.

With his back turned from Sophie, a hoard of shadows grabbed Sophie and swept her away. They were stationed out of touch but within view of Pierre.

The weight of shade's words hung in the air; the promise of freedom was tempting. With growing courage Pierre turned to the shadow and spoke, "Promises? From you? Your words are lies; it's what best describes you. How can we trust you?"

Shade gurgled with dark echos, "Ah, trussht. Sssuch a fickle thing hmmmm? It is in my besshht interessht to see you two fly away from here. The keeey,however sshtays."

"And what's to keep you from following us, ensuring that we never tell this tale?" Pierre asked, sensing something was off. He noticed Sophie out of reach in the trees near the edge of the Hollow Hills, slithering wisps of shadows holding her back.

"My young, feathered friend, you undereshhtimate me. If I wanted you ssilenshed, you would have been whishhpers long agggo. Now, the key!" Shade growled, his patience wearing thin. "You have losshed your only bargaining piecsh. If you care about your shhister, I... need... that... key!"

Realizing the plans had now changed, Pierre set off for the opening of the Hollow Hills. Knowing the shadows would follow, he held up the key and for all to see, laid it out on an ancient, weathered stone, and flew off.

Shade and his followers moved with incredible speed toward the prize. Stopping feet away, Shade motioned for the release of Sophie, they would deal with the two intruders later.

Sensing the momentous occasion, he paused before answering, "So you all can witnesssh the greatnesssh of my leaderrrsship, how I was the massshtermind that made this moment posshhible, and of course now, my reign over thissh land in fulfillment of the ancient prophecy." His spooky essence leaned down toward the key, and with one touch, he would be crowned as rightful ruler by Pomona herself.

The creatures who dwelt in the ancient woods, the ghostly beings, the ghouls and werewolves from the Halloween celebration, Crooked Straw and Luna appeared to watch as the thin, translucent veil between the two worlds was lifted. The first vision was of the Aos si, the magical dwellers of the hollow hills emerged, their unusual presence was almost dreamlike. They moved around the entrance to the burial mounds in a strange Celtic dance. Sensing his moment, as the goddess Pomona was rising from the mound, Shade took ahold of the mesmerizing artifact, the key to the Samhain treasure at last was his. As his nebulous form twisted with evil delight, it just as fast turned to horror as the key began to disintegrate into dust.

"NOOO!" he spit out of his grotesque face. At that moment, the fires burned bright inside the hills as the Aos Si opened the portal to the depths. Pomona with a flick of her hand, the shadows in all their putrid glory were drawn deep into the depths of the 'Otherworld'.

As the goddess turned to face her living subjects, Archibald emerged from behind the crowd of beings,

both living earthly creatures and those not on this side of the veil.

Pomona lifted the ageless crown, adorned with Sardis, Onyx, and Sapphire, placed it on his head, handed the scepter of the realm to him and proclaimed for all to see and hear. "Before you stands the true and rightful ruler of this realm. Honor him and follow him without reservation." She then leaned into him, whispered in his ear, and then vanished into the mound of the Sídh. The mystery of her existence now confirmed for all who witnessed the sacred ceremony.

The fires of the Hollow Hills were fading as dawn approached. The celebration of the ages was beginning as the sunlight shined on a new day. Archibald glanced up at the top of the trees, gave a thankful nod, touched his paw to his now royal chest and bowed to the pair of gray birds.

Perched high in a tree overlooking the hills, their hearts swelling with pride, the two weary birds gazed upon the vast kingdom below. It bustled with the noise of celebration and joy that now enveloped the land. "Sophie, do you see what we've achieved?" Pierre murmured; the triumph clear in his voice. "Let's go home." Sophie replied with fatigue in her voice, "I'm ready."

On their flight back to the vast pumpkin field, crossing over the flooded forest bottom and high over the whispering woods, their memories were full of the events of the past weeks. Their questions surrounding their missing family still not answered, they both found peace that they would someday find them. They knew there were many journey branches Babu held in their future. The humble confidence in their abilities and wits had grown immensely on this quest.

The pair landed on a rail near their first meeting with Crooked Straw. They gave a quick glance at the old pole he was tethered to, looked at each other and found an ever-growing love and appreciation for each other.

Flying to the decaying pumpkin, still with an image of Pierre's face on it and taking a deep breath, they began to feel the profound weight of their triumphs. A weight they would happily carry and remember for the rest of their days. They settled on a vine, and with a rush of wind and a whisper, they were gone.

— The End —

About the Illustrator

Jamie Ruthenberg is a Detroit-born author and artist, with a rich past in writing, illustrating, publishing, and education. She has published various works of fiction, nonfiction, and poetry, and has taught the beauty of the writing and art process to a range of students, from kindergarteners to graduate students. As a self-taught artist, Jamie creates her illustrations with a number two pencil and watercolor paint. Today, Jamie lives in Clarkston, Michigan with her comical rescue cat, Ella.

About the Author

---◆---

Curtis Lind, a former teacher, has transitioned into the enchanting world of children's literature, fueled by his extensive travels across Asia, Russia, Europe, and the dynamic center of Africa. His books reflect the profound influence these journeys have had on his life and the wealth of experiences he's accumulated. The Congo, with its vivid landscapes and extraordinary wildlife, has become a wellspring of inspiration for his writing. Curtis' stories are a beautiful interplay between his global adventures and the boundless creativity of young minds, forming the very soul of his literary works.

www.ingramcontent.com/pod-product-compliance
Lightning Source LLC
Jackson TN
JSHW040814310126
97339JS00001B/1